Doubletake

Sutton Miller

Clocktower Books

San Diego, CA USA
www.clocktowerbooks.com

Doubletake
by Sutton Miller

Clocktower Books

San Diego, CA USA
www.clocktowerbooks.com

Copyright © 2000 by Sutton Miller

CLOCKTOWER and design are trademarks of C&C Publishers.

Cover art by A.L. Sirois

ISBN 0-7433-0058-0

Prologue

Saturday, July 29—Dallas

Dusty stairs, shrouded in shadows, groaned in protest under his weight.

Fourteen steps to the top. Six more to go.

His right hand slid across the rough, peeling banister and the harsh rattling in his chest faded, replaced by a tremble of apprehension.

What if someone else has been here since...

Forcing his mind to blank out that possibility, he opened the door and smiled. The room was exactly as he'd left it.

The intruding streetlight cast eerie ghost-like slashes across her bare form and the dancing quality of the light mesmerized him. Against his will, his gaze was held then transported back to the grisly scene that had played only twenty-four hours before with him in the lead...

He had been participant and spectator alike, until his brain seethed with a terrible hatred that jangled the very bones of his massive skull. His hands tore into soft flesh as he repeatedly slammed her limp body to the floor. Then her neck snapped with an audible crack When the body gave its final death twitch, he relaxed his fingers. Trembling hands wiped a river of sweat and tears across his face as he gazed at her. Madness filmed eyes didn't see the horrid death mask.

"You really are so beautiful." He ran his fingers through long chestnut hair, stroking it into some semblance of neatness. "There. That's better, isn't it?"

He hunched over the body, his mind switching crazily between reality and a foggy area of fantasy. Suddenly, a voice wailed at him. It seemed to come from the face in front of him: a face that no longer held any beauty but loomed like a buzzard waiting for its share of the spoils. It released a vile gush of abuse, damning him, mocking him, and castrating him.

He covered his ears in a vain attempt to block the voice, but it didn't stop. "You weren't even worth the moment it took to make you..."

"Noooo!" He cried, staggering into the fetid bathroom where the dank, dirty walls echoed his misery. "It's not my fault. I never meant for anything bad to happen. Ever."

As suddenly as it had come, the anger subsided, leaving him in a state of deathly calm. It was the only right and just thing he could have done

He splashed cold water on his face and methodically dried himself with a well-used towel, careful to avoid the dark brown stains embedded in the cloth.

Closing the bathroom door softly, he stole one last look at the woman's body, now mottled in death. "You look lovely in yellow," he said.

Thursday, August 31

Releasing the air in slow spurts from his buoyancy compensator, Brad followed the grapnel guide rope to a pre-determined twenty-foot mark.

One, two, three, four...breathe. One, two, three, four...breathe. So still. So quiet. Can't use more air than everybody else. Slow down. Three to four foot visibility? Hell! Looks more like three to four inches.

Brad relaxed his tense muscles as he reached the marker on the rope. His breathing no longer came in short, frightened spurts and his ears had finally lost the piercing pain present before equalization.

This isn't so bad. Just a huge old pool, that's all.

Eyes now adjusted to the cloudy, yellowish water, Brad made out the vague forms of several large boulders below. *Must have been thrown there during the excavation that created this man-made lake.* He'd been waiting weeks for the opportunity to play here.

Brad checked his depth gauge where the red needle quivered over the twenty-foot line then he tugged once on the guide rope to signal the next diver.

He felt something brush lightly across the back of his knees and turned awkwardly to see what it was. His movements only served to tangle his legs in yards of bright yellow, nylon rope. He fought the urge to shoot to the surface.

Don't panic. Fear drowns. Just stay cool. Use what you learned.

The diving knife felt natural in his hand as he slashed at the strong, slender rope.

Man, if ol' Fox could see me now.

He reached further down toward his ankle and felt something soft and—

His teeth clamped down on the hard, rubber mouthpiece, trapping the breath in his throat.

Rotted flesh gave way beneath his fingers and floated around him like bits of wet tissue. Tethered at the end of the rope was what had once been a living, breathing person.

Chapter One

Monday, October 4

Susan Delgrave woke and rolled over to look at the clock on Tom's nightstand. Five forty-five. What on earth was she doing awake at such an ungodly hour? Some strange sense of unease had brushed across her like a chill wind, bringing her fully awake, but she couldn't pin down the source. She lay listening for something, anything, but the house was quiet.

Almost too quiet.

Only Tom's soft steady breathing convinced her she was being silly. Everything was all right.

Still, there had been something.

Another chill made her shiver and snuggle deeper under the blanket, seeking the warmth of her husband's body. As she brushed against his back, he stirred and rolled toward her. She softly traced a pattern across the smooth surface of his chest and felt her own body respond, marveling at the almost mystical bond they shared.

The magic started from the first moment she'd met him in an English Literature class at Baylor and hadn't diminished since. A man of tender sensibilities, Tom was the final ingredient for Susan's total happiness. Recalling what measures she'd used in order to convince him of that, brought a smile to her face.

Leaning closer, she whispered, "Tom! Are you awake?"

"Who wants to know?" He opened dark brown eyes and grinned at her.

"The upstairs maid."

She moved her hands further down his chest. He drew in a sharp breath. "If you don't stop that in exactly three hours, I'll tell your mother."

Susan laughed. "She warned me that you might not respect me after. Guess I'll just have to risk it."

Tom slipped the straps of her gown over her shoulders, revealing breasts already eager for what was to come. He touched one peaked nipple and leaned over to kiss her. First her eyes. Then her cheeks. Finally her lips, creating a surge of passion that drew her so close she thought she could enter his very soul.

Then his lips were everywhere, searing into her chin, her neck, and her shoulders. Passion thundered through her body until it reached a fever pitch.

Oh! It was so good just to touch, to feel his hardness pushing urgently against the tiny mound of her belly.

His hands trailed fire across her whole body, caressing, teasing, urging, until...

"My, God, it's almost seven." Susan struggled free from the tangle of blankets and Tom. "Remember, I have to use your car again. Wish you'd call the garage. All I get is, 'sorry, Ms. Delgrave. We're still waiting on parts.'"

"For a small fee I might consider it." Tom stretched his large frame across the bed.

"Okay, Smarty. While you're considering, consider this. Shower alone with no hot water." She pulled free and ran to the bathroom, closing the door in his face.

Tom smiled, grabbed his robe and went to make coffee.

They pulled in front of Twin Lakes High School at seven fifty-five and Tom gave Susan a long, lingering kiss. She pushed him away. "What would Mrs. Temple think if she saw us now?"

"She'd probably say, 'My, my, my, that Susan Delgrave is one lucky lady.'"

"You're a mess," Susan said as Tom stepped out and slammed the passenger door.

He walked around the car and leaned through her open window where he had a clear view of her open coat and the lush roundness of the top of her breasts. He reached in and pulled her coat together, caressing her at the same time. "Watch it, kid," he said in an affected Bogart voice. "You'll incite some poor bum to take advantage of you." He kissed his fingers then touched her cheek.

She smiled. "Better hurry or you'll be late."

Walking up the pitted sidewalk to the front of the school, Tom decided he had to be the luckiest man alive. He greeted the gray-haired Mrs. Temple with a bright smile. She tightened her lips and narrowed her eyes. He continued toward his classroom, making a mental switch from lusty thoughts to the assignment he'd give the English Composition students.

The feeling of unease returned as Susan pulled the Buick into the garage. A faint, niggling little fear prickled the hair on the back of her neck, making her feel slightly foolish.

What kind of mother would I be if I'm afraid of bogeymen and sounds that go bump in the night?

She smiled at the prospect of motherhood. There was no doubt in her mind that life was growing inside her. All she was waiting for was the final confirmation this afternoon. Tom had no idea. He didn't even know she was taking the day off to see Dr. Wallace. It would all be revealed in a surprise she'd planned for tonight.

After a dinner that would make Martha Stewart proud, Susan would give Tom the news. She knew he'd be delighted, even though it was a bit sooner than their timetable. But no way would he not want this baby as much as she did.

She reached for the sliding glass door, and her hand faltered when she noticed the door was open a scant inch. *Were we in that much of a hurry? Should I be afraid of what might be waiting for me?*

That thought brought an urge for laughter. *No more Stephen King novels for you until after the baby is born.*

She gave the door a tug and it rolled smoothly on the runner. Then she pushed the heavy drape aside and stepped into the den. It took a moment for her eyes to adjust to the dimness, and in that time of near-blindness she felt a breath of that indistinguishable fear again.

Something's wrong.

She stopped by the side of Tom's recliner.

Yes. There it is again. A faint whisper of sound. Whisper or rustle?

She whirled as something dark and heavy descended on her. It happened so quickly, she only caught a glimpse of a figure before she was engulfed in darkness. Some coolly impassive part of her mind registered a familiar flash before the quilt's oppressive weight, along with her own terror, pulled her to the floor.

"Oh my Go-" She tried to scream but the dusty odor of the blanket consumed her breath. She felt her stomach lurch. The sour taste of vomit filled her mouth and nose. A cold knife of fear twisted inside while her mind frantically searched for some reason.

Why is this happening? Is he going to kill me?

No! I don't want to die.

She heaved her body violently, struggling for breath and struggling to dislodge the terrible weight.

Hope died when a terrible pain exploded in her head. A blow smashed her face, filling her mouth with the acrid taste of the blanket mixed with her blood.

The certainty of her fate hit her as hard as the physical blow, and she tried to scream again. All sound was lost as a final darkness, a final shroud washed over her.

Chapter Two

Monday, October 4—Twin Lakes

Determination and persistence usually paid off for Detective Barbara Hobkins, but not this morning. This morning she was still bogged down in a burglary investigation that should have been routine. It was the sixth day.

"Damn!" She slammed the notebook on her desk and stood up, smoothing the wrinkles on her Khaki pants.

Across from her, Keith Reeves, engrossed in his own muddy water, looked over. "Going for coffee?"

"Yeah."

"Bring me some?"

"Who says I'm coming back?"

Keith smiled, an act that turned his craggy face into tolerant amusement. She recognized it as his way of telling her he knew better.

Barbara walked slowly down the hall to the break room, trying to clear her mind for a fresh approach. Since they'd broken that burglary ring a few years back, it hadn't been so easy to tie everything up in a neat little package. A proliferation of drugs brought more chaos to what used to be somewhat organized and predictable.

Maybe I should shuck it all and make my parents happy.

Remembering their shock when she'd first announced her desire to be a cop, Barbara didn't fight the urge to smile. She knew they both had assumed she'd just grow out of it. Even though while all her friends were playing Barbies, she devoured every mystery in the library and listened to the police scanner with her Uncle Bob.

She'd been about eight when she first voiced her interest in police work, but her father had registered the same shock when she'd walked into his office after making her application to the Twin Lakes Department. His response had been no big surprise. "You've only been out of college a week. Why not give yourself some time?"

"I don't need any more time." She squared her shoulders and regarded his imposing presence. "Besides, it's too late to reconsider. I've already applied."

Breaking eye contact, her father had taken a moment to run his pudgy fingers through his mop of white hair. She'd often wondered what thoughts had gone through his mind during the delay.

"Guess a debate is out of the question," he'd finally said. "So what do you want from me?"

"I know I'll be accepted. No problem there. But I'll need your help with mother. You know what a fit she had last time I even mentioned the possibility."

Barbara hadn't thought of that in ages. So much had happened in the last eight years that it felt like the conversation took place an eternity ago.

And she was slightly amused at her early naiveté. *Why on earth did I think Mother would be the hardest obstacle I'd face?*

Despite changing attitudes and government mandates to include more female police officers, her first years with the TLPD had been the pits. Originally confident of an immediate slot in criminal investigations, she'd shouldered one disappointment after another. Chief Broyles had been more inclined to assign her to deskwork or routine patrol, neither of which offered many investigative opportunities unless she counted tracking the occasional lost Fax.

Her big break came three years ago when she'd blustered her way into a juvenile case. The suspect was a fourteen-year-old boy caught on a B&E. Royce Wertco. She'd never forget that name.

Barbara had suspected from the beginning that the case was more than that one-time excursion into criminal activity. Hours spent talking with the gangly teen with the surly attitude, reinforced her belief. He'd been overly defensive and protective of a couple of eighteen-year-old dropouts with a long list of priors.

The investigation eventually exposed a burglary ring profitably operating out of a pool hall for over a year. The leader, a nineteen-year-old dropout with a long-standing drug problem and an attitude, recruited young boys like Wertco to keep him supplied for a percentage of the take. The eighteen-year-old held the exalted role of 'business manager.'

Barbara was enraged that the most vulnerable could be sucked in so easily. Without outside influence, Wertco probably would be a good kid. So she'd testified on his behalf, and he pulled a first-offense-probated sentence.

His two friends hadn't been so lucky. They'd gone to prison.

She'd expected Royce to be grateful for helping him, but he'd turned on her. "You hung my friends out to dry." He'd screamed. "Now what am I supposed to do?"

"Straighten yourself out. Go to—"

"Yeah, right. A real fuckin' Mary Poppins we got here."

Looking into his cold, blue eyes, Barbara had experienced the hollow feeling of being hated for the first time in her life. The hatred was so strong, it seemed to fill the already stuffy courtroom and made it harder for her to put him out of her mind.

A short eleven months later, Wertco served his own time. "Six months in reform school ought to teach the little bastard something," Keith had said. "Bet they don't waste their time coddling his ass in Dallas either."

Barbara had borne the snide remark in silence, but Wertco's conviction for assault hit her like a personal defeat. Somehow she should've been able to reach him that first time. Turn him away from his self-destructive path before it swallowed him whole.

She'd beaten herself up about that for a long time.

"But it won't happen again."

Barbara didn't realize she'd spoken aloud until the uniformed officer beside her turned with a questioning expression. "What?"

"Nothing."

The officer spooned a generous portion of sugar into his coffee and moved on. Barbara filled two mugs then headed back to the office.

Okay, Hobkins. No more mothering. Put your emotions in a bag. Stay detached.

Weaving her way down the crowded hallway she wondered if the pep talk would work.

Chapter Three

Monday, October, 4—4:45pm. Twin Lakes

By the end of the school day, Tom found he was still feeling good and somewhat philosophical as he walked out into the bright afternoon sun. He couldn't even complain that Gene had cancelled the morning review with no explanation. He was too intent on getting home to question the oddities of his boss and his friend.

Things had been so good between him and Susan lately Tom almost couldn't believe it. The fact that they'd survived the first few awkward years of marriage and now found themselves in a mutual state of respect and happiness was a constant source of surprise. Sometimes he wondered what he'd done to deserve someone like Susan.

If they ever made it until they were ninety, to look back over a life rich with memories, it would definitely be to her credit, he realized, not his.

Maybe he could learn. Maybe, as the years marched on, the delicate emotional act of total loving would become second nature to him as well. But until then, Susan was the strength of their relationship. Susan, with her laughter, her spontaneity, and her penchant for surprises.

Tom suspected she'd been working up to another one recently. Part of his suspicion had to do with a little gleam in her eyes or a secret smile when she thought he wasn't looking. He'd seen it this morning and almost asked her about it. But the press of time had halted his words. He'd ask when he got home.

Thinking about it made his heart beat a little faster. He surely did like her surprises.

At the garage, he got the same evasive story about waiting for parts that Susan had received. *Damn! Why didn't I ask Gene to wait?*

Sighing, he tuned out the attendant's apology and contemplated calling Susan to pick him up. *Screw it. I'll walk. The exercise'll be good for me.*

He cut through the park and broke into a slow jog, enjoying the fresh autumn air. A few kids clambered over large barrels and up a ladder to the slide. Watchful mothers sat on benches ringing the play area. If his guess was right, Susan would be here in a couple of years.

A block from home, he slowed to a walk again and felt the relief from muscles too long dormant. *Have to do something about that. Maybe take up softball again.*

Heading up the front walk to his house, he paused to snag a piece of paper dancing across the lawn on a light breeze. *Or I could do some of the yard work. Make Susan happy.*

He stuffed the paper in his pocket, opened the door, then stepped into the foyer. Inside, he paused again as he picked up a faint, sour odor. He stood for a moment, testing the air then fought an impulse to laugh. Last week Susan had accused him of turning into a birddog since he'd quit smoking. Just because he could tell something was rotten in the refrigerator before he even opened the door.

This smell was different. It made Tom's skin crawl, triggering alarms he hadn't felt in ten years. The faint but disturbingly distinct stench of fear, sweat, and death made him forget for a moment that he hadn't just entered the jungle in Columbia where his unit had rousted drug dealers.

Tom's mind whirled with crazy possibilities as his body automatically took over and moved him through the tile entryway with footsteps soft as a cat's.

What if Susan comes out of the kitchen and finds me stalking through the house with an umbrella held at ready? He tried to be amused by the thought but couldn't shake the feeling of apprehension clinging like an insistent leech. A thin trickle of sweat rolled down his back as he moved into the den.

The smell was stronger. Tom felt it crawl up his nose and invade his brain.

Every sense was alert for the slightest sound, the slightest breath of movement, but all was still. Too still. Then Tom froze. In the twilight dimness that cast the room in weird shadows, he could barely make out a vague, lumpy shape on the floor in front of the sofa. Something that didn't belong there. It looked like an oversized doll, carelessly thrown aside when a child had tired of playing with it.

There was even a blanket.

Oh my Go- Tom raced the last few steps and bent down to pull the edge of the blanket aside. It was—*Oh, God, noooo!*

He fought for control as the reality banged in his head, demanding to be acknowledged.

Suddenly the dam burst. Reality won, and he saw the trail of blood from her swollen, split lips. The trail ran down a battered cheek and pooled in the halo of blonde hair. Eyes registering every detail, the pain was so intense he clutched his stomach to keep his guts from spilling out. He sank to the floor, trying not to look anymore.

But his eyes kept going back.

Each time, they saw something else. The unnatural cant of her legs. The mottled flesh...the blanket...no, a quilt. *Our quilt. Someone used our...*

"Nooooo!" The scream resounded through the empty house like a gong. On and on it went, while he held himself together and rocked.

An eternity later, he pulled himself up on shaky legs and took a hesitant step forward. He needed to feel something besides the gut-wrenching pain but nothing would come. He knew there were things he shouldn't do. Just like he knew there were things he should be doing. He only wanted to die.

The quilt will smother her. Got to do something about the quilt.

Tom's rational mind told him he shouldn't touch anything. He'd watched enough cop shows on TV to know that much. But the part of him that loved Susan couldn't stand to see her that way. He went into their bedroom, the jumble of bedding a harsh reminder of the morning.

Don't think about that.

He pulled a sheet off the bed and talked himself into walking back to the den. *You can do this one last thing for her.*

It seemed like another eternity passed before he could summon the courage to remove the quilt. As it pulled free, waves of nausea rolled over him and he swallowed hard to hold back the bile. He covered her with the pretty flowers she liked so much. Then, hating himself for having to do it, he ran to the bathroom, his stomach heaving.

By the time the retching subsided, Tom's mind and body were numb. He leaned against the cool porcelain of the tub. What was he to do? *I don't know. My God, she's.... Nobody told me how to act when...*

A sudden, strong urge for a cigarette obliterated everything else. He wiped his mouth with the back of hand and stood on trembling legs. He made his feet move toward the bedroom. "I'll call Gene. He's my friend. He'll bring me some cigarettes."

Police Chief David Broyles answered the phone on the first ring.

"We got ourselves a bad one." A male voice trembled with urgency.

"What's up, Richards?" Broyles took a sip from his perpetual cup of coffee.

"Homicide. 4207 Seely. School teacher's wife. Strangulation, rape, looks like. Friend of the family called. The husband found the bo- "

"On my way." Broyles slammed the receiver down and knocked over a stack of folders in one swift motion.

"Shit." He bent over and gathered the papers then slapped them back on his desk. "Margaret! Get Reeves and Hobkins over to 4207 Seely. Pronto."

Two black-and-white units marked the address, their roof flashers emitting space-like lasers of red. A large crowd gathered on the front lawn, the lights rendering them zombie-like.

"Goddam vultures," Broyles muttered, heaving his bulk out of the car. Every time he made the squeeze between seat and door, he swore he'd go on a diet.

"Get these maggots out of here and call for more help," he ordered Richards who'd hurried to meet him.

"Right, Chief." The young man hustled toward the crowd, a sense of authority straightening his back and putting a spring in his step.

Broyles slicked back the straggles of brown hair that had been lifted by the wind then walked toward the open front door of the brick ranch house.

Inside, he noted that the floor plan was identical to his own house that was located only a few blocks south. A coming-home feeling crept up his spine as he walked across the marble-tiled entry. Even the same crappy wallpaper, geometric gold foil leaping out like some rabid circus beast.

Guess they haven't done much remodeling either.

Straight ahead in a doorway to the left, Broyles saw patrolman Clifford Vaughn standing sentry over the den. *Standing sentry or scared stiff?*

A look of relief washed across the slight patrolman's ashen face as Broyles pushed past him. Vaughn nodded in the direction of the body.

The room was a typical tract-house living/den. A stone fireplace huddled beneath a heavy oak mantle, glistening dark paneled walls looked over beige carpeting, kitchen on left, patio beyond. Almost strategically centered on the floor was the sprawled body of Susan Delgrave.

Broyles had seen his share of death during his twenty-six years on the job. Accident victims, drownings, suspicious deaths, murders, but it never got any better. Never got any easier.

As a young patrolman back in Arizona, he'd written his first letter of resignation after encountering his first death. He'd followed the same procedure for the next three years. His own personal panacea for death. Privately resigning time after time, death after death, seemed to make the dreams diminish. Dreams in which the victims were rowed, platoon-like with empty-socket eyes and outstretched arms, begging him to help. The whole scene encased in a silver shell of 'whys.'

Pushing the distraction of private thoughts aside, Broyles walked to the middle of the room, then stopped and meticulously took in every detail with a visual sweep. He'd learned about details the hard way when he'd superimposed his fingerprint over a killer's bloodied one by simply flipping a light switch. A very costly and embarrassing mistake he'd never forgotten.

The victim lay on her back, legs grotesquely bent, as if trying to hide her shame. Slender, bruised arms were folded protectively across her chest, the stiff fingers appearing to grasp at the pink tee shirt. Chalk-like, reedy tendons held what was left of the almost severed head. Her eyes, mottled and glazed with death, were filled with a paralyzed, hopeless terror.

And despite all his protective measures, Broyles felt a softness attack his knees. He turned abruptly to Vaughn who'd stepped up beside him. "Who found her?"

"Husband. He's in the back bedroom. Only he ain't in too good'a shape."

Gene Wilkins, high school principal, bachelor, and the man in control at all times, found himself up against something he couldn't handle after he hung up the phone. Telling his story to the police in a faltering voice, he'd felt like a bit actor in a second rate movie. Now, his only desire was to get to Tom as quickly as possible.

Halfway out the door, he turned and went back for another pack of cigarettes. He had a feeling they were going to need them.

In the garage, he opted for the sedate SUV over his Mustang. Somehow the occasion called for black and conservative.

The agonizing drive to the Delgrave home worsened with the sudden eruption of a rainstorm. One minute the sky was merely gray. The next, huge drops splattered the windshield with such force that Gene had no choice but to pull his Explorer against the curb. Thunder roared and lightening split the sky, releasing a torrential downpour. Hail pinged off the roof and hood, then bounced crazily on the concrete like marbles dumped from a sack.

Every second of delay gnawing at him, he watched a drunk stumble for cover beneath a cheap awning and momentarily envied the drunk's simple life. Nothing to worry about except where the next drink was coming from. Nobody to be responsible for. Nobody to worry about. And nobody to mess up his life.

Not that his life was so bad anymore. He did his job adequately. Didn't care about advancement any more. Just get through to retirement. He'd only had ambition when he mattered to Nancy. When it became clear that was no longer true, he'd decided that nothing much in life mattered any more.

Glancing out the windshield, he realized the torrent had eased to a drizzle. Anxious to move away from his morbid thoughts, Gene pulled into the street, catching one last glimpse of the drunk through the slapping windshield wipers.

Good luck, Buddy.

He felt a mounting sense of dread as he neared Tom's street, and it got worse when he turned the corner and saw the house. Despite the rain and the efforts of the police to keep the area clear, a crowd of thrill seekers milled in an atmosphere of shared excitement.

Gene had to park three houses away. He locked his car, dropped the keys in his pocket and hurried through the rain and the crowd. At first, he thought the police weren't going to let him in. A patrolman stopped him the minute he approached the front walk. He explained his presence to the young man who looked like he should be at the high school football game, not the scene of a murder.

"I'll have to check with the detectives," the officer said. "You can wait here."

Gene stepped under the meager protection of the small porch where an overhang reduced the drizzle to a fine mist of moisture. He thrust his hands into the pockets of his blue Windbreaker and waited.

Finally a large, beefy man, reeking of power and authority, came out of the house. Gene noticed that the man was sweating profusely, despite the cool evening breeze. His lips were white and pinched.

"Chief Broyles." The man took Gene's hand in a bear-like grip. "You the one who called?"

Gene wiped the moisture off his face and nodded.

"Why not the husband?"

"He asked me to. Said he just couldn't."

The other man studied him for a long moment and Gene held his gaze steady. "Can I go in?"

Again the long scrutiny then a slight shift. "Okay. But stay out of the way."

Gene caught a glimpse of the activity in the den as the detective hustled him through, judiciously keeping his large frame between Gene and the body. It didn't matter. Gene was numb. Had been for some time now.

Entering the bedroom to see Tom huddled on the loveseat, Gene was struck at how shrunken he looked. His friend barely acknowledged his presence with a momentary flicker of vacant eyes. Broyles mumbled something about being back shortly and left.

Gene lit a cigarette and held it out. Tom took it automatically, choking on the first drag. "Susan would kill me if she caught me smoking again."

Attempting a weak smile, Gene sat down. The silence was deafening. What could he say?

A few minutes later, Broyles came back in and nodded toward Tom. "How's he doing?"

"Okay, I guess." Gene moved closer to the detective. "I think he's in shock."

Broyles walked over and touched Tom's shoulder with surprising gentleness. "Mr. Delgrave. Sorry to have to do it, but I have a couple of questions."

Tom nodded.

"Did you or your wife expect any visitors today?"

Tom shook his head.

"No repairmen? Anything like that?"

Again a slow negative movement, like a marionette in the hands of an inexperienced puppeteer.

Broyles hesitated, then sighed deeply before joining Gene by the window. "The rest of the questions can wait."

"Can I take him out of here?"

"Yeah." Broyles glanced back toward Tom. "Might want to take him by the hospital. Get something to knock him out. Once the shock wears off, it's going to be a bitch."

Gene followed the detective's glance, then nodded. "I'll take him to my place after."

"Leave your number with Detective Hobkins before you go."

Tom offered no protest about leaving. He stood and took the jacket Gene held out, every movement as slow and deliberate as a robot performing a mindless production-line task. Then he waited for Gene to take his arm and lead him out.

The long hallway unfolded like some carnival mirror maze. Gene couldn't stay focused. *Detective who?* He couldn't remember the name Broyles had given him. His hand sought support from the pimpled plaster wall.

He silently cursed his evasive control and lack of...lack of what? *Shit. Lack of everything*. Only once could he ever remember feeling so inadequate. The night Nancy asked for a divorce. No. Not asked. Told him. He'd known for months that their marriage was doomed and part of him wanted the divorce despite sporadic efforts to make it work. Even so, the guilt had been unbearable, the 'ifs' clouding all logical thoughts. She'd left him with nothing, slashed through his feelings, leaving him as exposed as white bones peeking through a wound.

He'd known what she was like from the beginning, but he'd overlooked her emotional maliciousness, wanting to believe she was perfect. He'd almost convinced himself she was. Then he'd discovered the hard way. No one's perfect. Had it been her failure or his?

"Mr. Wilkins?" A soft voice intruded on his thoughts. "I'm Detective Hobkins."

Gene ran an unsteady hand through his dull, brown hair. "Hobkins. That's right. Detective Hobkins." He felt foolish when the repetition registered, but the woman didn't seem to find it odd. She offered him a firm handshake and a tentative smile.

"Tom will be at my place." Gene fumbled in his wallet for a card, aware of deep-set eyes appraising him. Bright emerald eyes framed by a halo of copper hair. About Susan's age.

The woman tucked the card inside a notebook and turned her attention to Tom. "I'm very sorry for your loss. We'll be in touch tomorrow."

Then she disappeared into the den and Gene wished he could call her back. She'd been a momentary anchor and he was drifting again.

Chapter Four

Tuesday, October 5—Twin Lakes

Barbara shrank from the hulking form coming at her. *No. Please. Don't! God! I don't want to die.*

She felt an abrasive scrape across her cheek, and a scream of naked terror rose in her throat. An instinct of survival made her swing her fist in a wide arc, and she screamed again as she connected with something solid. Then she was awake, sitting up in bed. Her body trembled as she tried to shake the remnants of the nightmare floating in the pre-dawn dimness. The nightmare in which she'd tasted the hell Susan Delgrave must have experienced. The nightmare that left her feeling naked and vulnerable, prompting her to reach for the Beretta in the nightstand.

She'd touched something. *That wasn't part of the dream.*

When the dresser resumed normal proportions, no longer looming like some giant monster ready to pounce, she eased her bare feet to the floor, carefully scanning the room for that 'something' she'd touched.

In the dim light, she saw a whitish form huddled in the corner. *Oh my gosh. Charlotte. I must have socked her a good one.*

Barbara knelt beside the badly frightened cat, who regarded her with eyes heavy with accusation. "Come here, puss." She put the gun on the floor, then reached out and smoothed the fur disturbed by alarm. "I didn't mean to hurt you."

The cat responded to the soothing tone, allowing Barbara to lift her into her lap. She realized her nightmare had somehow gotten tangled with Charlotte's morning ritual of face washing. But that was probably of little consolation to the cat.

Barbara soothed Charlotte for another few minutes, then put her gun back before heading to the shower. Dressing didn't take long: jeans, a silk blouse, and a charcoal blazer. Her latest haircut had been wash-and-wear, so she was ready in less than fifteen minutes. Five more minutes to pour food for Charlotte and brew a cup of instant, and she was ready to walk out the door.

She carried the coffee to the car in a thermal mug. A good dose of caffeine would chase the rest of the cobwebs away.

Still a bit shaky from the nightmare and the after effects, Barbara welcomed the slow pace of the early morning traffic as she eased her Datsun onto Main Street. It was a doublewide stretch of road cutting through the center of town, two lanes going east, two going west. Strip malls, clusters of small businesses, gas stations, and fast-food joints lined the road on both sides. Anything the small town consumer would need neatly packed into five miles of commerce.

"Problems? Call 569-1411." The radio announcer's voice made Barbara smile. "You got that right," she said.

It had been a long time since a victim had gotten to her like this and she wondered why. She was definitely not a skitzy female given to unreasonable fears, and she'd long ago learned to disassociate from the horrors of crime scenes. *So why this? Why now?*

Because the victim was so close to her own age? Because the woman's life had been so obviously what Barbara would never have? It wasn't that she didn't want to make her mother happy and have a family. She just needed to find a man who wouldn't try to make her into something she could never be.

Anne Murray's voice came across the radio, filling the car with fairy-tale words and sweeping Barbara's thoughts to Roger. "You Needed Me" was his favorite song. He wanted so desperately to be needed that their relationship was cracking under the strain.

Barbara sang the words and let her mind explore the problem. Why couldn't she enjoy the pedestal he had so lovingly placed her on? Roger was everything a woman could possibly want. Handsome. Virile. Successful. And he loved her. But there was something missing. Missing on her part apparently, but still a void.

Lately he'd become more demanding of her time. Little things at first. She overlooked his sudden 'I was in the neighborhood' visits for over two months before suggesting he call first. Hurt feelings evolved and their last date had been an effort. She swore Roger actually brooded over the Porterhouse at Austin's Steakhouse. That's when she'd realized he was 'OVER' everything. Overprotective. Overgenerous. And over-demanding.

She absently touched the solitary diamond nestled in the smooth hollow of her neck, realizing that that train of thought would take her to places she didn't want to go. Better to keep her thoughts on the case.

Easing her Datsun into a parking space in the lot adjoining the low red-brick building housing the Municipal Offices of the city, Barbara turned off the ignition and took a deep breath. *Focus. That's all it takes.*

She passed the Licensing Bureau, City Clerk's office, and headed toward the back where the TPPD had its little corner of the world. She was just sitting down at her desk when Keith Reeves sauntered into the small cubbyhole of an office they shared.

"Morning." He balanced his large frame on the corner of her desk. "You want to talk to Delgrave? Vaughn's going to get him."

Barbara contemplated the man, who, with the same indifference that Charlotte had exhibited that morning, was wrinkling the reports on her desk. Keith was a large, bear of a man with skin so fair it had a faint translucent quality. He worked hard to appear close-shaven, and his blue eyes held an intensity born of years of practice. That intensity could cut through the bullshit any perp threw at him.

He cleared his throat, reminding her that he was still there.

"Sorry," she said. "My mind was off somewhere."

"A female trait I'm well acquainted with."

Barbara refused his bait. "I'll take Delgrave. He'll need someone with a little more compassion than you're known for."

"That so?"

"Yeah. You can handle good old Dr. Davies. He gives me the creeps."

Keith gave her a mock salute and heaved his bulk off her desk. After he was out the door, Barbara allowed her first smile for the day.

Dr. William Davies' office could easily qualify for Federal disaster assistance. Mounds of frayed file folders and books, guarded by several abandoned cups of coffee, covered his ancient wooden desk and every other surface in the room.

How does the guy keep track of anything?

Already on his second cup of brew, Keith carefully shoved a stack of papers aside and choked on the billow of dust his action created. He eased his throat with another swallow of coffee and took a seat on the faded paisley couch, prepared for the inevitable wait.

Being the Dallas County Medical Examiner for thirty-three years had given Dr. Davies a crusty, no-nonsense shell seldom penetrated by anyone, and he had a reputation for not caring who he left waiting in his office. Keith remembered a story regarding the commissioner and his ill-fated attempt to have Davies dismissed. The Doc's response had been, "Fine, I'll go to LA." The city officials had suddenly decided to scrap the commissioner's request.

Keith raised his cup to the absent Davies, "You go, Doc."

Thirty minutes later the diminutive Dr. Davies bustled into the office. With a curt nod he extended his smooth, pink hand. "Detective Reed?"

"Reeves, Sir."

"Yes. Well. The preliminary report's here somewhere." Davies shuffled papers across his desk. The action almost created an avalanche before the doctor pulled out a file. "Adams?"

"Delgrave. Susan Del..."

"Delgrave. That's right." He stirred the precarious pile again, then pulled out another file and opened it. "Here it is."

Amazed, Keith watched the unusual facial movements of the old doctor as he read the report. Eyes rapidly darted east and west while his cactus-needle eyebrows followed a north/south course. When Davies looked up, Keith felt a flush at being caught staring and reached for his cold coffee to cover.

"Officer Reed," The doctor addressed the side of Keith's head. "This is only the preliminary report. I'll do the full post later today. Then it will take a few days for the forensic serologist to do his tests."

Keith considered correcting Davies again, then decided the effort would be fruitless. He listened as the doctor read from the report, "Death was caused by a double fracture of the cricoid cartilage. Stated more simply," here Davies looked at Keith, "the ring of gristle that forms the upper part of the windpipe. Immediately below the larynx in the front of the neck. A common fracture during strangulation."

Davis paused to scan the page, then hold it out. "I believe the rest is self-explanatory. Now if you'll excuse me, I have a class waiting."

"Thanks, Doc," Keith took the report. "Chief Broyles will be in-"

He suddenly found himself talking to the door. "Like I said, Doc. Thanks a lot."

Chapter Five

Tuesday, October 5—Twin Lakes

After making the necessary phone calls to the school, Gene went to check on Tom, who was tangled in a mess of arms, legs, and bedding. He was relieved to find his friend still sleeping. That gave him a chance to have coffee and come to grips with the whole situation. There were times it was still all shrouded in so much unreality Gene was waiting for a director to yell, "Cut." He was again playing his mental denial game.

That's absurd. You can't wipe reality clean like a used blackboard. You've got to face it. Deal with it. And survive.

Resolving to do all he could to insure Tom's survival, Gene returned to the kitchen. God knows, he owed him that much.

Tom awoke slowly, small sections of his mind coming to consciousness at their own pace. Feeling groggy and disoriented, he looked around, not recognizing the framed Remington prints on the wall or the brass lamp on the night table.

Where the hell am I?

Then it all came back in a succession of mental flashes like a macabre slideshow, the most recent being brought here by Gene. The memory of what had happened earlier brought waves of pain that crashed against his heart in a merciless onslaught. He considered succumbing to the misery but didn't know if some fragile part of him would break in the process. Instead, he forced his body out of bed and padded to the shower where he adjusted the spray to allow icicles of water to assault his face.

He winced at the soreness in his left arm. The minor pain brought another memory of a glistening tiled room, a young man in blue scrubs pushing a plunger, then layers of soft, gray mist. A mist that had gently cradled Susan just beyond his reach.

No. Don't think about that.

Tom dressed in jeans and a Chambray shirt he found on a chair by the closet. Both were too big and he had to roll the cuffs. Under the shirt was an unopened pack of cigarettes. Without consciously deciding to, he put them in his pocket and went out to face... *Face what? Susan's gone. What's left?*

"Hope my clanking didn't wake you," Gene said as Tom walked in looking somewhat like a scarecrow in the ill-fitting clothes. "Want some breakfast?"

"Just coffee." Tom slumped in a chair at the maple table, and some disassociated part of his brain noted the overhead light glistening in the glossy finish.

Gene brought a mug over and set it down. Then he got his half-finished waffle and sat down across from Tom. "You okay?"

"As long as I don't think. My head feels like it's full of broken glass."

"I called Susan's folks."

Tom winced at the sound of her name, and Gene turned quickly away. Tom nudged him. "It's okay," he said. "We can't go the rest of our lives not saying her name."

"Yeah, well..." Gene averted his gaze again, then cleared his throat. "Called the superintendent, too."

"Appreciate that. And all... well, you know."

Gene got up and squeezed Tom's shoulder before walking to the sink with his dirty dish.

I understand. Everything will be okay. That's what the touch meant. *Dear Christ. Sweet, suffering Christ, why did this happen? How could it happen?* A shudder of agony shot through Tom as he pictured Susan's body. His thoughts locked on to the way she'd died. What pain she must have felt. Or maybe the terror was worse. Is there a separate arena for terror and pain? What were her last thoughts as...?

He forced his mind elsewhere. *God, think of anything but the way she died. Anything.* His junior and senior students were due to take the SATs. When? Some of them had so much trouble with simple sentence structure. He should help them. But when was the test scheduled? The all-important date was too elusive.

Tom fumbled in his pocket for a cigarette, glad his friend had his back turned and couldn't see the tears warming the edges of his eyes and sliding down his cheeks.

The sudden peal of the doorbell jangled every nerve in Tom's body, and he wondered when, or if, there would ever be a time when he didn't jump at every noise. As if sensing the need for reassurance, Gene touched his arm on the way past. "Be right back."

Tom wiped the beads of perspiration from his face, listening to a muffled exchange from the other room. Then Gene returned with a short, thin man a step behind. "This is Officer Vaughn."

"Hate to intrude, Mr. Delgrave." Something in the officer's voice rang with sincerity. "You need to come to headquarters with me. Just a few questions. Won't take long."

"Let me get a jacket." Tom stood, surprised at the calm that came over him. He felt like he was on a fucking carnival ride that had suddenly stopped at left him in a deathly quiet.

But at least it was better than the pain.

Barbara stopped by the Chief's desk after talking with Tom Delgrave. Broyles held up a finger while he ran another one down a report he was reading then glanced up. "Get anything?"

"Not much. Same tune as last night. Everyone loved his wife. No angry students seeking revenge for a failing grade. No enemies. Not a clue as to why someone would do this."

"What about the medical report?"

"Keith went over there this morning. You know how long that can take."

Broyles' smile was a surprise. She couldn't remember the last time she'd seen one. "What does the friend have to say?" he asked.

"Let you know in a couple of hours."

Broyles nodded, dismissed her with a wave of his hand, and turned back to the mountain of papers on his desk.

Gene was surprised when his doorbell rang again. Tom had called from the police station to say he was going to see Susan's parents, so it couldn't be him.

When he opened the door, it took a few moments to recognize the young woman standing on his porch as the detective from the night before. His impression of her then had been numbed. Today the sunlight shimmered off her coppery hair and he saw a splash of freckles across her nose. She reminded him of one of his students, fresh, eager, and expectant.

Barbara opened her tan jacket to reveal her shield. "May I come in?"

"Of course." Gene stepped aside so she could enter, then directed her toward the living room.

She swept the room with a practiced eye. It was almost austere in its lack of decoration, yet there was a peacefulness in the fireplace adorned with antique cast-iron utensils and crowned by a massive oak mantle. Books spilled out of the bookcase in the corner and current issue of Time graced the low table in front of a plush, leather couch.

"Would you like something to drink? Coffee?"

"No, thank you." Barbara sat on the edge of an occasional chair. "This shouldn't take long."

Gene sank into the softness of the sofa and waited while she pulled a small, tired-looking notebook out of a pocket.

After establishing the standard "who, what, where, when" of the interview, Barbara took a moment to organize a train of questions then led with, "How long have you known the Delgraves?"

"About five years. Tom came to Twin Lakes High shortly after they were married."

"Did you know them well?"

"We're close."

Barbara hesitated briefly. "Did they have any marital problems?"

"No."

She wondered about the abrupt shift to one-word answers and decided to push a little. "You sure?"

Gene rose abruptly and paced, finally turning to face her. "I don't know if you seriously think that Tom could have done that-" He made a vague gesture with his hand.

"We do look at family first," Barbara said. "Even the mystery writers know that much."

Gene considered her for a moment then sat down again. "I'm sure they had problems. Everyone has problems."

"Was she faithful to him?"

He glanced quickly away and Barbara wondered. "Do you know something?"

"No... I..." He met her eyes. "This is hard."

"But necessary, Mr. Wilkins." She gave him a moment, then continued. "Can you think of anyone who might have had something against the Delgraves? Any threats at school?"

"Nothing. Wish I could point a finger at a suspect, but..." He let the thought fade and stared at the Berber carpeting.

"What about his life before he came here?"

"Don't know much. He was in the service. Did some stuff in South America he doesn't like to talk about." Gene paused, brushed a piece of lint off the arm of the sofa, then glanced back at her. "Doubt that had anything to do with this."

"What about the wife? Could there be something from her past?"

"I really don't know much about that. I think she grew up in Indiana then her parent's moved here. She and Tom met at Baylor."

"Were you at the school this morning?"

The question seemed to jerk him upright. "Uh, no. Took some personal time. Went into Dallas to drop some information off at the NEA office."

Barbara sighed and closed her notebook. She shouldn't be that disappointed. It wasn't like she'd expected him to hand her a suspect and a motive. But it would've been nice.

"That'll be all." She stood. "Appreciate your help, Mr. Wilkins."

She extended her hand, and his return handshake was a pleasant contrast to the limp-fish attempts she usually received. When he didn't break the contact right away she was surprised that she didn't mind.

"I feel a little foolish," he said, finally releasing her hand. "I kept forgetting you are a woman."

The comment unsettled her, and she gave him an appraising look. Was that a compliment on her technique, or was he hitting on her? And why didn't she mind?

Needing the professional boundaries, she pulled out her card and handed it to him. "If there's anything, anything at all you think of that could help, call."

Driving back to the station, Barbara considered the subtle shift that had taken place at the end of the interview. Had she misread it? No. She could still feel the warmth of his touch. *This is ridiculous. Not to mention unprofessional.* But she couldn't stop her mind from exploring the interest that had been sparked.

The most surprising part of it was that he wasn't even her type. His softly planed face and thinning brown hair were in direct contrast to the rugged 'cowboy' types she preferred. But there was something appealing in his presence. She couldn't deny that. His eyes were fascinating, changing expressions as he talked. They'd almost smoldered in intensity at times, turning them the shade of rich, dark chocolate then softened to a velvety quality at others. *Doe eyes? Is that what they're called?*

A loud honking jerked her from her reverie. She almost stalled the car in her haste to get through the intersection. She'd better spend more time thinking about the case and less time thinking about the color of a man's eyes.

Barbara was just hanging up her jacket when Keith stepped in the doorway. "Chief wants us in the conference room, STAT."

"Right behind you." She picked up a handful of reports and followed his lumbering gait down the hall.

"Okay. Let's see what we've got so far." Broyles leaned his buttocks against the edge of the table and waited while patrolmen and detectives shuffled in to find seats. "Vaughn?"

The officer flipped open his notebook and read as if dictating to a machine. "A Mrs. Ruzio across the alley says she saw the Delgraves leave around eight that morning. Saw the victim return about a half-hour later. Alone. After that,

Ruzio went to another part of her house. Never saw anything else. The rest of the neighbors were either gone to work or still asleep."

"Wish I had a choice like that," Keith muttered.

"Can it, Reeves."

Barbara took note of the edge in Broyles' voice. Obviously he was going to be all business this afternoon. He fulfilled her mental prediction when he addressed his next question to Keith as if the interruption hadn't occurred. "What do you have?"

"Preliminary report from Dr. Davies." Keith took out a handkerchief to mop the sweat beading on his forehead. "Cause of death, strangulation. But he did call with an interesting update during the post. The victim was pregnant."

Barbara's professional aloofness crumpled at Keith's words. Suddenly it was much too easy to imagine what Susan Delgrave must have felt. The husband didn't know. Barbara was sure of that. Their earlier conversation had exposed a man shattered by the loss of a wife. The news of a child added to the loss should finish what was left of his life.

"What about forensics?" Broyles asked.

"They're still working on the quilt," Barbara said. "But the husband did say it looked like one they had. It'll take a while to eliminate all the trace fibers that belonged at the scene."

"Okay," Broyles said. "Are you liking the husband at this point?"

"I don't know, Chief. We can't stop looking at him. But I'll be damned if I can come up with a motive."

"What if the kid wasn't his and he knew it?"

"I'd bet my life he didn't even know she was pregnant, let alone question paternity."

"But do we *know* that?"

Barbara bit back the first response that came to her lips. Broyles had made it clear on numerous occasions what he thought of her intuition. "My conclusion is based on the fact that neither the husband or the friend mentioned a pregnancy. It would be a big deal, especially with the husband. So I stand by my opinion. But that doesn't mean I won't check with the woman's doctor."

"Anything new from the friend?" Broyles fished a half-chewed cigar from his coat pocket and examined it.

Barbara had to stifle a laugh. The smoking ordinance had been in place for five years now, and he still kept forgetting. She waited until he looked at her again before answering his question.

"He backed up the husband's story but couldn't verify what time Delgrave arrived at school. Wilkins didn't come in until about noon that day."

"He have an alibi?"

"Says he was in Dallas. It'll be easy to check."

Everyone in the room seemed to be waiting for the Chief's next question. When it didn't come Barbara plunged on. "I think the killer is probably an outsider. Not family. Not friends."

"We still have a lot of ground to cover." Broyles took a swallow of coffee from the Styrofoam cup he'd carried in. "It's too soon for opinions."

Barbara sat up a little straighter. "We're not exactly rolling in suspects."

"What are you getting at Hobkins?"

"Maybe we should run this through the Behavioral Unit at Quantico."

"We're not crying psycho yet." The Chief's voice was cool. "We've done our best to keep the details from the press. You know what will happen if we start slinging 'psycho' around."

"We don't have to *sling* anything." Barbara worked hard to keep her voice controlled. "But we have to look at the possibility of a serial killer. Even a crime of passion wouldn't have been carried that far. Remember what..." For a moment she lost her composure, then compressed her lips into a firm line. "A burglar caught in the act, a husband who found his wife cheating, would not do what was done to Susan Delgrave."

"You've made your point, Hobkins," Broyles said. "Let's just keep it under wraps. We don't want a panic."

"Fine. As long as we all recognize that there could be a very sick person out there."

Chapter Six

Friday, October 8—Twin Lakes

Dressed in a somber, dark suit, Gene walked slowly toward the park, oblivious of the beautiful fall morning. Normally he found it invigorating to be out in the early morning freshness and often walked the two miles to school so he could, as the song said, "stop and smell the flowers." But not today. Today he wasn't going to work. Today they were going to bury Susan.

Tom, with her parents' permission, had decided on a simple graveside service, abandoning the idea of a wake altogether. Enough ghouls were already crowding around. Tom's house looked like a tourist attraction, and after one night he'd sought refuge back at Gene's. There was no sense in inviting more intrusion.

Gene had assured his friend that Susan would have approved of the simplicity.

He brushed a few crusty brown leaves off the wooden bench and sat down, overcome for a moment by a deep sense of anxiety. *How am I going to get through this? How could anyone?* It had taken months for Gene to get over losing Nancy, and he'd at least had some choice.

A flicker of movement caught his attention, and he watched a small flock of sparrows dig in the lose dirt under a tree, using the focus to keep his mind in the present. He needed to keep his head clear. For Tom. For himself. For the days and weeks ahead. It wouldn't help to think about Nancy and that terrible time of discovering she didn't love him anymore.

Barbara and Keith came to the cemetery that morning, too. They came, not as mourners, but with the vague hope of turning up a lead. It wasn't at all unusual for a killer to show up at a victim's funeral. The detectives would run a trace on every license plate in the parking lot: part of the dull routine never glorified on television.

The morning sun, filtered by a gauze-like mist, cast hazy shadows across the mourners, who were shrouded in jackets and coats of black. Their stiff postures indicated the depth of the human tragedy playing out on that slight rise.

Watching the pallbearers march solemnly to the grave and slide the casket onto the brace, Barbara felt a prickly sense of unease. A picture of the victim's body presented itself vividly in her mind, and some of the suffocating panic of her nightmare caught in her throat.

"You okay?" Keith asked. "You don't look so hot."

Barbara flashed a half-hearted smile. "Must be that lousy instant coffee."

On the surface, he seemed to accept her explanation, but she had to turn away from his penetrating gaze. "Come on," she said, turning down the last row of cars. "Let's get the job done."

Coming to the end, Barbara stopped and looked toward a battered pick-up parked on the grass, well away from the other cars. She couldn't tell if gray was the truck's original color, or if it had just faded after too many years in the elements. She squinted against the sun to check out the two men lounging against the truck. From a distance, they looked like any of the men she'd busted for drunk and disorderly at the Lone Star Grill when she'd been on patrol.

She motioned to her partner. "See those guys?"

Keith shaded his eyes. "Look like real winners, don't they?"

"Let's find out what they're doing here."

Keith led off, and Barbara followed, stepping carefully on the loose gravel on the edge of the parking lot. Her unease increased as they neared the truck, and again she found herself stepping carefully, this time around headstones. *What's wrong with me? Haven't been afraid of ghosts since I was a kid.*

The man sitting on the hood of the truck turned pale blue eyes toward the detectives. He was bigger than the other man, with unwashed hair and unwashed clothes. Barbara fought an impulse to pull back as Keith flashed his shield and asked the men what they were doing there.

"Just waitin' for things to be over." The man nodded toward the huddle of people at the graveside. "Then me an' Jimmy's gonna close things up."

"You work here?" Barbara asked.

"Not regular." He flashed a boyish smile that didn't quite reach his eyes. "Work for the city. Me an' Jimmy just do it on the side."

He made a digging motion and again, Barbara felt an urge to step back. This guy was a creep, but maybe that was a job requirement.

She studied them both for a moment, but there didn't seem to be any point in asking anything else. Catching Keith's attention, she turned and headed back toward the parking lot.

"Ugly bastard, huh?" he said when they were far enough away that the men couldn't hear. "Must go with the turf." He laughed and pulled at his wrinkled collar.

Barbara didn't join in the levity. The morning was taking its toll. Her nerves were stretched tighter than strings on a guitar, and she wondered how soon they would snap. First, she couldn't banish the image of Susan Delgrave as she'd looked in death. Now, talking to the guy who'd cover the body left her cold inside. She'd never thought about what happens after the mourners leave.

How stupid to think the shiny casket, smothered in flowers, would cover itself.

She'd read somewhere about man's unique ability to psychologically soothe the unpleasantness of events by subconsciously writing one's own ending. The acceptable epilogue. Death ends at the funeral.

How convenient. What's the point of going any further? Why look for the gravediggers? Why research the body-moldering process seventy-two dark inches beneath the ground?

She glanced back at the truck, wondering if the chill that swept over her was the result of her morbid thoughts or that strange man's insolent attitude. "Come on." She slid into the car. "Let's get out of here."

Chapter Seven

Thursday, October 21—Twin Lakes

Keith, caught in the usual morning rush of traffic, looked across the street at the deserted park. Deserted by children, families, dogs, Frisbees, and fathers, leaving empty benches and lonely silver swings. The dismal scene reminded him that he hadn't spent a single hour with his children since the murder. His mind automatically rejected any event or person not associated with the case. His wife, Brenda, had begun to wonder at the completeness of his fixation.

"You know what's happening to you?" she'd said at breakfast this morning while Keri was absorbed in a book and Keith Jr. looked on in solemn interest. "What's happening to us? You never talk about anything but this murder."

"It's all I can think about. You don't know what will happen if this thing stays in pending. Years from now, every time there's a murder even remotely similar, we'll have to butt in. We'll have to know." He'd felt the piercing presence of his ulcer and stuck a thumb into the sore spot. "It's driving us all nuts. But for all the effort, we're no closer to finding the killer than we were last week."

"You'll get him, Daddy." His son said and Keith found a small measure of comfort in the endorsement.

After Brenda scooted the kids out the door with lunch money and book bags, she'd poured him another glass of milk and gently kneaded his shoulders. It had been a silent message of understanding, and he still felt the lingering comfort of her touch. Quiet, easy-going Brenda had been his whole life for twenty-one years, and despite his independent exterior, Keith Reeves knew where his real strength came from.

The kids had come late, after they'd almost given up on the possibility of a family, and he almost felt guilty. Why did he deserve to be so blessed when people like Tom Delgrave got the worst of life's curses?

Pulling into the station parking lot, he realized he'd never find an answer for that question. Life was a paradox more often than not, so he might as well quit trying to figure it out. He eased his Bronco into the space next to Barbara's bright blue Datsun. Almost space. Years of bitching about her sloppy parking had been in vain.

His grudging acceptance of her as his partner three years ago had been the cause for many behind-the-back snickers from other officers, but the snide remarks had failed to generate the desired response. Keith enjoyed his few months of center stage before the other guys caught on. In the long run, she'd turned out to be a damn fine cop, and a lot easier to look at early in the morning than the other clock-stopping mugs.

Inside the station, he nodded to Barbara, shed his coat, and headed toward the bathroom. She followed his progress down the hall, covering a smile with her hand. Then she sucked in her cheeks: the first telltale sign of suppressed hysteria and lowered her head to study the mounds of paper on her desk. She counted the seconds until Keith came storming back, his neck and face a funny shade of purplish red.

He stopped just outside their doorway and waved a hand to encompass every-one within close proximity. "Who's the wise guy?"

The demand was met with averted eyes and complete ignorance, punctuated with a few snickers.

"This is it!" Keith looked about ready to explode. "From gilded plaques to personalized toilet paper. I've had it. Do you hear me? I've had it."

Barbara looked at him, and he knew her smile was anything but innocent. "What are you yelling about?" she asked. "Someone would think you have a prob-lem."

Muttering, Keith turned away. It wouldn't do any good to push the issue. He'd been trying to get them to lay off for years, but no amount of protest made any difference. *Never should've told them how hard it was to live in a one-bathroom house with a teenage daughter and a wife.*

He went back into the bathroom and tossed the flower and candle in the trash.

Gene heard the door to his office open and looked up to see Marsha Bennet poke her head in. "Interrupting anything?" she asked.

"Just winding things up for the day."

"You got a minute." Marsha closed the door. In a dress, she could've passed for a librarian, but the shorts pegged her as a PE teacher.

"Sure." He waved her to a chair. "What's up?"

"I'm not sure. It seems a little silly. Might be nothing more than a childish prank." She lowered her lithe frame into the chair and crossed muscular legs. "Someone's been going through the lockers in the girl's shower room."

"That doesn't sound silly."

"It's happened several times since school started, but stealing doesn't seem to be the motive. Whoever's doing it passes up money, jewelry, CDs."

Gene absently searched his pockets for a cigarette and settled for a stick of gum. "Has anything been taken?"

"Panties."

"Like in underwear?" He stopped with the gum halfway to his mouth and stared at her.

Marsha nodded, her blunt-cut auburn hair brushing her shoulder with the movement. "That's why I thought it was a prank at first. You know how kids are. 'Let's take Janie's panties and hide them.' But one of the girls found hers today." Marsh hesitated just a beat ,and her expression was etched in concern. "They were slashed."

Gene leaned forward intently, leaning his elbow on the desk. "She's sure they're hers?"

Marsha nodded again. "They were a gift. A special gift."

"Where are they now?"

"In my office." She glanced away then back. "Didn't want to touch them more than I had to."

Gene rummaged in his desk drawer and came up with a rumpled brown lunch bag. "Get them and bring them back."

Marsha touched a finger to her lips as a realization appeared to dawn. "Guess I should've come to you sooner."

"It's okay. Sometimes we need to pretend that school is the way it used to be."

"That's the problem." Marsha grabbed the bag. "It'll never be completely safe again."

While he waited for her to return, he debated whether he should call the police. But was this really a crime? Maybe it would be better to just drop by with his story and the torn panties. Then the professionals could decide if it's important or not.

And it will give you a good excuse to see a certain detective again.

He had to think about that for a minute. Wasn't that like stepping out on a frozen lake in an early spring thaw?

Well, sometimes you've got to live dangerously, Gene, Old Boy.

He stopped at home and traded the Explorer for the Mustang.

Gene turned the car toward the front parking lot of the Municipal Building and eased into an open spot. He took the bag, locked the car, and headed toward the door, hoping no one would stop him and think he was some kind of nut who goes around with panties in a brown paper bag.

Inside, he saw a counter with a uniformed officer behind it. The tall Hispanic man was talking to a teenage girl with spiked hair and so many earrings Gene wondered how she could hold her head up. He considered waiting until the officer was finished, then followed a sudden impulse. He stopped a patrol officer who had just emerged from a rabbit warren of cubicles to the left of the front desk. "Where can I find Detective Hobkins?"

"Down the hall to your left." The officer pointed past the cubicles. "Second doorway. Can't miss it."

"Thanks."

Stepping through the open door, Gene saw two desks facing each other. The first one was unoccupied. Barbara sat at the other one, twisting a strand of hair while talking on the phone. "I know I promised, but..." She looked up, shifted the receiver and held up one finger. "I'll see you Friday then." She hung up and turned to him. "Mr. Wilkins. What brings you here?"

"Not interrupting, am I?"

"No. I was just going for coffee. Want some?"

"Sure. If it's no bother."

Barbara disappeared for a few minutes, then came back with two steaming mugs. "Hope you like it black. I didn't think."

"That's fine." Gene accepted the mug and waited until she was seated, noticing the scoop of her knit shirt and the glitter of the diamond in the hollow of her neck. It was stupid to even consider asking her out. Stupid on a lot of levels, but one was most obvious. Someone had given her that piece of fine jewelry, and it might be the same someone she'd just made a date with.

"I assume you didn't just drop by for a cup of coffee?"

Her question pulled him back on track. "It may be nothing," he said. "But something came up at school."

"Oh?"

"But I'm probably wasting your time with it. Probably should've just left it at the desk."

Barbara leaned forward. "Why don't you tell me and let me decide?"

She sipped her coffee and watched him thoughtfully as he related the story. She found his slight blush endearing. Poor man had trouble actually saying the word, 'panties.'

When he described the condition of the underwear, she forgot her amusement and her coffee. Unrelated as the incident might be, her psycho theory came to mind. At this point, she was willing to grasp at anything. "Do you have the panties with you?" she asked.

Gene reached into his jacket pocket and handed the wrinkled sack across the desk.

She glanced inside, then punched a button on the phone. "Vaughn. Come here for a sec."

The officer stepped into the office and Barbara handed the bag across her desk. "Take this to the lab."

"Can they get anything from them?" Gene asked after Vaughn left.

Barbara's slim fingers rolled a pencil lightly across the desk. "Sometimes. You never know. Seems we spend most of our time not knowing much of anything. Then something breaks and we drown in possibilities."

She dropped the pencil in a mug filled with an assortment of pens and pulled one out. "I need the names of the girls involved. And, if possible, the dates panties were missing."

"I only have one name, Sarah Billingsly. Those were hers." He made a vague gesture in the direction Vaughn had gone. "Marsha could give you the names of the other girls."

"Is this Sarah in Tom Delgrave's class?" Barbara looked up from her notebook.

"I'm not sure. I could go back and check."

"Tomorrow will be soon enough." Barbara stood and offered her hand. "Thanks for coming by."

Gene stepped into the hallway, thinking about the feel of her hand and the flash of her smile. *Damn.* He couldn't just walk away. He turned and went back in. "Can I ask another question?"

"Sure." Barbara paused with her coffee cup halfway to her lips.

"Would you have dinner with me tonight?"

She dropped the cup so fast the brown liquid slopped over the side, splattering the papers on her desk. She grabbed a tissue and mopped the offending mess then glanced at him. "This is quite a surprise, Mr. Wilkins."

"Under the circumstances, I'd rather you call me Gene."

"What circumstances?"

"Dinner."

"What makes you so sure I'll accept."

"I don't know," he said, a slow smile transforming his face into something soft and appealing. "My natural charm? Hunger?"

Barbara laughed. "This is absurd."

"No it's not. Crazy perhaps but absurd? Never. What time do you get off?"

"Six."

Gene glanced at his watch. "It's five-thirty now. I'll wait outside. I'm driving a purple Mustang."

He watched an expression of amazement take shape on her face and shrugged. "What can I say? A holdover from my wild and impetuous youth."

"You don't strike me as the impetuous type."

"You'd be surprised."

"I'm not sure this is a good..."

He held up a hand to stem her words. "Just think about it. I'll wait outside."

She watched him walk out the door, then sank into her chair. What on earth was he thinking? *What am I thinking for even considering it?*

She tried to concentrate on filling out the time sheet, but her eyes kept straying to the clock where she watched the minute hand move slowly toward the top. Maybe it wouldn't hurt to go out with him just once. His story checked out so he's not a suspect. Might not even end up being a material witness. But to be on the safe side, we'll keep it to one date.

Barbara smiled at this regression to adolescence when the merits of potential dates had been endlessly debated before making a decision. Then, the debate had been verbal and held with Stacy Overton, the girl with the most experience in ninth grade. She'd always advised the girls to go with their hormones.

In that case. I certainly hope Gene wasn't joking.

Outside, she glanced around the parking lot until she spotted him. He did have a purple Mustang. He waved through the open window, motioning her over.

"Nice wheels," she said, stopping about a foot from the car. She swept the interior with a quick glance, noting the black dash and charcoal colored seats before turning her gaze back to his casual smile.

"I only bring it out for special occasions."

"Pretty sure of yourself, aren't you?"

"Not really." There was a momentary flicker of seriousness in his eyes before he smiled again. "Just hoping."

Barbara hesitated before walking around and getting in the other side. "I should go home and change."

"You're fine." He waited for her to buckle up, then backed out.

"Where're we going?"

He checked traffic before pulling out, then glanced at her. "How do you like your hamburgers?"

"You're taking me to McDonalds?"

Gene laughed. "No. A place that makes hamburgers they way they're meant to be."

"I'm disappointed. The least I expected for our first date was candlelight."

"Maybe next time."

Barbara returned his smile, a bit surprised at how much that possibility appealed to her.

He watched them drive away, momentarily frustrated. Course, maybe it was better this way. He didn't know what wild hair had brought him here in the first place.

Sipping his beer, he tried to figure out what to do now. *Shouldn't do nothin', asshole. She ain't done nothin' to you. Leave her alone.*

But he didn't want to leave her alone. He wanted to play with her a bit. Maybe not any more than that. He'd see. But definitely play. *How else can I get some fun out of life?*

A small smile touched his lips as an idea took shape in his mind. He could go to her place. Maybe leave her a present. The anticipation stirred his most primal instincts. The hunter stalking his prey. *There's no hurry. I've got time. An abundance of time.*

He'd be careful. Very careful. Like a surgeon slicing a delicate artery. He'd learned not to be sloppy. To stay in control. He could do anything, and the cops couldn't stop him. *A bunch of smartass pricks chasing themselves in widening circles.* They never knew who he was, or where he was.

He pulled into the shadows in front of the apartment house. Getting inside wouldn't be a problem. He was a master at slipping in and out like a fleeting shadow.

What to leave behind?

Nothing definite. Nothing to give him away. Just enough to show he'd been there. Then wait. Wait and watch the frightened eyes darting around for the enemy, never sure of when or where he'll appear. But knowing. Always knowing he'd be back.

The vivid picture produced a dichotomy of pleasure and revulsion. An uncomfortable bulge formed between his legs, threatening to steal his control. *I'll take care of that later, too.*

By eleven, Barbara persuaded Gene to take her back to her car. As much as she hated the evening to end, she had an early meeting in the morning.

They'd talked their way through giant cheeseburgers dripping with condiments, ice cream, beer, potato chips, and a few cups of coffee. Not necessarily in that order. She'd had a marvelous time.

So marvelous, she hadn't thought about the case or anything else all evening. *Not even Roger.*

That was a sobering realization. He wouldn't be pleased to know another man had entered her life, even temporarily.

Barbara shrugged and stuck her key in the lock on her apartment door.

That just might be a nice problem for him to have.

Pushing the door open, she flicked on the light and dropped her purse on the old library table she'd confiscated from her mother. She stood for a moment with a sense that something wasn't right. Then the absence of Charlotte registered. The cat should have been here, protesting the long hours of being cooped up alone.

That's strange.

Barbara walked into the living room. No cat snuggled on the throw pillows on the sofa. "Charlotte," she called, heading toward the kitchen. "Where are you? Aren't you starving?"

Silence made the skin crawl on the back of her neck. There was no way the cat could have gotten out of the apartment. That meant she was hiding or...she was... *Oh, God, she couldn't be dead.*

Maybe she'd been closed in the bedroom that morning.

Barbara raced down the hall, trying to keep the fear at bay. She knew it was absurd for a grown woman to act this way about a cat. But Charlotte was the only warm, loving thing in her life right now that was constant.

Anxiety intensified when she came to the bedroom door. It was open.

"Kitty, kitty, kitty," her voice started out calm but quickly rose to strident. "Where are you?"

The faintest of sounds responded from under the bed. Barbara grabbed the flashlight from her nightstand and lifted the dust ruffle. The beam of light bounced off two yellow slits in the far corner, where Charlotte crouched in a fuzzy white ball.

"You crazy cat!"

Her relief at finding the car alive was short-lived as the full realization of finding her huddled under the bed hit her. The only time Charlotte acted like this was when a stranger had been in the apartment, especially a man. The cat had hidden for three days the first time Roger had been there.

Did that mean...?

Other than Charlotte's strange behavior, Barbara hadn't noticed anything unusual the first time through the apartment. But then, she hadn't been looking either.

Taking her little Beretta out of the bottom drawer of the nightstand, she checked the load then went back through each room with a skittish Charlotte at her heels.

A careful search turned up two things of interest. One could be explained by Charlotte's habit of jumping on shelves. The body powder was knocked over in the bathroom. The dampness in her shower and the unnatural angle of the showerhead defied logic.

Someone's been in here.

Barbara allowed her consciousness to accept that fact, and a small lump rose in her throat. Somehow this small sign of intrusion was more disturbing than if she'd found the place ransacked or someone to shoot.

She put the gun on the counter and reached for the phone.

A squad car showed up less than five minutes later.

After lunch the next day, the Chief called Barbara into his office. "Just read the report from last night," he said. "What gives?"

She gave him the story from beginning to end, omitting her fear for the cat. He watched with a thoughtful expression.

"I don't like it," he said. "No sign of forced entry? How'd he get in?"

She knew the implication of that question. It was one she'd already thought of. "I'm changing the locks today."

"Good."

Broyles took a cigar out of his pocket, and she wondered when he'd stop carrying them inside. After a moment, he put it back. "We'll run the prints. See what comes up. But there is one thing..." His voice trailed off in an awkward silence.

"Yes?"

"Vaughn got something from the drain. Checked it out himself instead of waiting for Crowder to fit it into his crazy schedule. You know Vaughn and his penchant for science."

"Yes?" Barbara asked again.

"He found some hair. Male." Broyles took a sudden interest in the cigar in his pocket again.

Barbara wasn't sure, but she thought he was blushing. "What do you want to know?" she asked with wry amusement. "When was the last time a man took a shower at my place?"

"Exactly." His voice was firm.

She adjusted her tone to match his. "Over a month ago."

"That long?"

Barbara found his surprise amusing but decided a verbal answer might steer the conversation toward places she didn't want to go. Especially not with her boss. She deflected the question with a shrug.

Broyles sighed and leaned back in his chair. "I've made arrangements for extra patrols in your area."

"I can take care of myself."

"Yeah. Well, humor me."

She nodded, then waited for whatever was next. He rocked gently, appearing to be deep in thought.

"That all?" she asked.

He dismissed her with a wave of his hand. "You be careful with the new keys."

"Yes, Sir."

"Save the smartass routine for your partner."

Barbara bit back the smile as she rose and gave him a mock salute.

Chapter Eight

Friday, October 22—Twin Lakes

Aimee's breath came in short, harsh gasps as she raced around the track. A long plait of russet hair thumped on her back in perfect rhythm with the slap of rubber soles on the dirt. The late afternoon sun drenched her in sweat. She suppressed the pain assaulting her body and forced her legs to move. The pressure of the upcoming meets caused her to push harder than usual. A week of precious practice had already been lost to a stubborn cold. She wasn't going to lose any more time if she could help it.

A junior at Twin Lakes High, she'd been running track for two years. She was a fierce competitor and had placed second in the state finals last year. Second wouldn't do this year. Next to her boyfriend, Tony, running was number one in Aimee's life.

"I'm second fiddle to a dirt road," was his favorite lament. But he was so sweet, and she loved it when he pouted. Or when he worried about her running alone so late it the day.

The pleasant fall weather allowed her to wear shorts and a light tee shirt, and the freedom allowed her to form a kinship with the wind. It was like they were one entity, sweeping around the track. There was nothing else quite so thrilling.

Her mind automatically dismissed the man watching her round the last curve. He was a common sight around the school grounds. Sometimes she was sure he had the power to appear out of nowhere.

She remembered that time after practice when she couldn't get the kickstand up on her bike. Using all her strength, she'd tried to slide the metal rod across the bent catch and into place but it wouldn't budge. Then she'd felt like an electric current had run up her spine. She whirled and collided with him. He was creepy. No getting around that. But he'd fixed her bike. Didn't do anything else. So maybe she was just letting Tony's worries get to her.

Gene carefully skirted the dirt piled on half the sidewalk and nodded curtly to the man who was planting trees. *Guess I'm not the only one who had to work late today.*

"Mr. Wilkins!"

He looked over to see Aimee waving from the chain link fence that separated the parking lot from the track. Her legs pumped as she ran in place and grinned at him. He squinted into the glare of the afternoon sun hanging low behind her. " It's late, Aimee. Shouldn't you be on your way home?"

"I will in a minute. But I wanted to ask about the office-aide job. You said you'd call."

Gene slipped his key into the lock and opened the door. "Sorry. I've been busy."

Aimee huffed a couple of breaths then slowed her pace. "I sure would like the experience."

"I'll have to let you know."

"Okay." The note of disappointment was unmistakable.

Gene hesitated. "Want a lift?"

"Got my bike."

"I don't like the idea of leaving you here." Gene glanced again at the sun, which had sunk lower on the horizon. "It'll be dark soon."

"I'll be okay. I do this all the time."

He hesitated again, then slid into the seat. "Don't be too long."

"Okay." Aimee waved and took off down the track.

Gene watched her fluid, almost effortless run for a moment then brought his engine to life and pulled out of the parking lot, his wheels sighing softly against the concrete.

After two more laps, Aimee collapsed in the grass and watched the sky darken from blue to gray to deep mauve. A light breeze dried the sweat on her tee shirt and cooled her at the same time. She listened to the beat of her heart slow closer to normal, and her thoughts turned to the brief conversation with Mr. Wilkins. It had been like so many others recently, short, almost to the point of being brusque. Like there was some kind of reserve between them. He used to be a lot friendlier. Had she done something?

Don't be silly. It started when that teacher's wife got killed. He's probably upset about that. And he did say he's been busy. No sense worrying about it unless he ends up saying 'no' about the job.

Satisfied, she stood up and brushed spikes of brown grass from her clothes. *Better get going. Still have homework to do before Tony comes over.*

She slipped into her warm-ups, hung her gym bag over the handlebars, mounted the bike, and headed north on High Creek Road.

Friday, October 22 was Aimee Nelson's last workout. She died at 6:03pm.

Chapter Nine

Friday, October 22—Twin Lakes

Barbara sipped her margarita and idly watched the crowd of dancers trying to keep up with the wild music exploding from the sound system. The Rooster's Roost was Twin Lakes' sole offer of entertainment for the younger set, and the place was always jammed. It had the same spangled façade of some of the Dallas nightspots, but under the glitter, it remained a renovated hay barn.

Most of the time she enjoyed it though. Barbara loved to dance, losing herself in pounding bass or slow, soulful melodies that invited intimacy between partners. Tonight she just wasn't in the mood.

"It'll do you good to be around normal people for a change," Roger said when she'd suggested a quiet dinner. He opted for the Roost.

She'd only agreed because it hadn't been worth the hassle of arguing. Her whole life had become one big hassle of late. *Problems at work or problems with Roger. Take your pick.*

Her feelings about him were riding a seesaw that had been more down than up the last few months. The strain was palpable. Of course, she blamed herself. The pressure of her job. Her changing values.

Maybe.

To give him his due, Roger hadn't changed and, as she looked at his broad, handsome face, she wondered if that was the problem. Roger was exactly the same as when she'd met him six months ago at a benefit for Special Olympics at the country club.

Then, she'd been impressed with his confident air and explained away the first hints she'd seen of his self-absorption. He hadn't become a successful developer by being benevolent or shy. Sometimes a person has to be a little obsessive, a little pushy, to make it.

So why couldn't she still see him that way instead of making mental lists of his personality flaws? She looked away before her face could give her away. *Why am I crucifying myself?*

It would be stupid to pretend she hadn't been affected by the wedding of her last single friend. That had been two years ago, and when Marcy called a few weeks ago to announce her pregnancy, it suddenly made the encroachment of forty more frightening. Could Barbara meet someone, fall in love, get married, and have a baby in the next five years?

She took another sip of her drink and glanced back at Roger who was sitting with an unreadable expression. Suddenly her eyes misted as she was struck with a stunning realization. *It's over.*

Part of her wanted to be relieved. She wouldn't have to endure the post-date agony of self-doubt any more. But it was hard to feel anything but sadness when she remembered that once, a long time ago, she'd cared for him.

Even now, the part of her that wanted motherhood wished that they'd been able to work things out.

"Where'd you go off to?" Roger's tone, like his expression, was unreadable.

"Oh." She offered a tentative smile. "Nowhere in particular."

"It's 'the job,' isn't it? That's all you have time for anymore."

Barbara sighed, a tiredness knotting her shoulders. "Let's not start that again. This is our first date in weeks. Couldn't we at least try to get along?"

"I've had plenty of evenings free."

His petulance made her want to scream or laugh... or both.

"When are you going to realize the truth," he continued. "If you'd lose that insane attachment to your job, we could have a normal life together."

A glitch in the sound system sent a scream of steel strings through the room, and Barbara grabbed the interruption like a lifeline. It gave her a moment to take a breath and find some tactful way of saying she had a headache. Then another noise intruded and saved her again. She reached in her purse and grabbed her pager.

She checked the number displayed and dug her cell phone out of her purse. Then she realized it was too noisy near the dance floor. She looked over at Roger. "Excuse me."

He shrugged and waved her away.

A few minutes later, she rushed back to the table. "There's been another murder," she said quietly. "I've got to go."

If the situation hadn't been so desperate, she would've laughed at his expression. It was almost triumphant, like he'd been waiting for an opportunity to prove she cared more about her job than him.

God, he doesn't have a clue.

Grabbing her denim blazer from the back of the chair, she was glad she'd driven her own car. She gave him one last look. "Goodbye, Roger."

He didn't respond.

The location dispatch had given her turned out to be a heavily wooded area just northeast of the high school. The lights from a crowd of black and white units flashed across the bare trees and tangled brush, making the scene look like the set for a horror movie. Richards waved her over.

Barbara nodded to the grim-faced patrolman and carefully made her way through the cordoned area. She shivered in the evening chill, wishing she'd stopped at home for a heavier jacket. Richards pointed, and she followed his gesture to the mutilated body of Aimee Nelson. Long, thin fingers seemed to be pitifully clinging to an old blanket.

Another chill shook Barbara's body and she averted her face.

Dead leaves and brush crackled behind her, and she turned to see Keith. "Christ, it could've been Keri," he said, anger blotching his face.

Before she could reply, he handed her the dead girl's school ID card. "Found this in her gym bag."

Barbara recognized the signs of too much association in the tremble of his hand. Better divert him before he broke. "Davies do a TOD?"

"Few hours, he thinks." Keith took a deep breath. "Couple of coon hunters stumbled across the body. Chief just left for the girl's house. Parents called about nine to report her missing."

A cold wind swept Keith's words away and rattled the brittle tree limbs overhead. Barbara strained forward to hear. She knew he'd soon start thinking of his daughter again, picturing her pink and white bicycle silently guarding a body in place of Aimee Nelson's. A heavy weight settled on Barbara's chest. *Too much is happening too quickly. Maybe Roger's right. Nobody who longs for normalcy should do a job like this.* A ridiculous thought. *Who'd do it if they don't?*

She cast about for something to focus on, and her eyes were drawn like magnets to the still form now being photographed. Each flash of Polaroid light brought out another aspect of the brutality inflicted on this poor girl. Barbara fought an urge to scream and rage at the demented thing that had done this. She held her elbows tight against her sides in defense of the cold wind and her rollicking emotions.

"Did you hear me?" Keith touched her arm. "Chief wants us at the house."

She nodded. "I'll follow you."

Keeping one eye on the taillights of Keith's Bronco, Barbara tried to compose herself. She was a professional and somehow had to stop identifying with these victims. She had to shove her personal feelings aside and stop grasping like some rookie at the nothingness of involvement.

Why did the thought of the break-in at her apartment keep intruding like a staccato rap in her mind? Why did she feel such a kinship with the victims? Was there a connection? Was she suppressing a warning? Had Susan Delgrave's killer familiarized himself with her house, her shower, her things...before?

Taking a deep breath, she forced the fear to a far corner of her mind and tried to look at it analytically.

Item number one to consider. A break-in at the Delgrave home hadn't been reported, but if it had been done like hers, would they have noticed? Without Charlotte's odd behavior, she wouldn't have.

Item number two. The faces of both victims had been mutilated. Psychological profile studies report face mutilation indicates familiarity.

Those are the facts. Not feelings.

Looking at the facts, she could keep her mind off the mental picture of that child nestled deep in brittle leaves and snarled brush.

At the Nelson's small frame house, Barbara eased her car between two black and white units, then followed Keith up the front walk to the door. Two flowerpots with dead geraniums stood on the little slab of concrete that was supposed to be a porch.

Inside, Barbara scanned the tiny entry, which had a wooden hat tree and no room for much else. The entry opened directly to the living room, and she saw Broyles in there with a young boy who looked like he'd rather be punching someone's lights out than talking.

"Who's he?" Barbara asked, pulling Vaughn aside and nodding at the wild-eyed boy.

"Victim's boyfriend, Tony Fields. Got here about the same time the parents did. Or so he says."

"Think he could be the doer?" Keith asked with a soft voice.

Vaughn considered for a moment, then shook his head. "Naw. Reactions are all wrong for someone covering. He's upset and madder than hell. But no sign of fear. No evasiveness."

Barbara took one last look at the boy, then crossed to the other side of the living room where a thin, gaunt man in his late forties sat with a small woman about the same age. She had the same color hair as her daughter, a soft dark wave that touched her shoulder. It was almost a final blow to Barbara's control that the couple was huddled on a loveseat. She swallowed the emotions that wanted to erupt from her gut and pulled down the shade to her soul. Then she walked over to them. "Mr. and Mrs. Nelson? I'm detective Hobkins. I need to ask a few questions."

The woman turned tortured brown eyes to Barbara. "My poor Aimee... my baby... why did this..."

Mr. Nelson pulled his wife closer. "I'm sorry," he said to Barbara. Then he squeezed his eyes shut and slowly rocked his wife.

The room was suddenly very hot, the stifling effect of human misery hanging like a heavy fog. Barbara wanted nothing more than to run from the pain as fast as she could. She was saved from that disgrace when Richards touched her arm. "Chief said to give you what I have."

Blowing out the breath constricting her throat, Barbara followed him into a small neat kitchen. He put his back to the refrigerator and pulled a well-used notebook from his shirt pocket.

"Call came in at 10:35. Hunters found the body. One of them tripped over the bike. Damn near fell right on top of her." He stopped to clear his throat, and Barbara was glad she wasn't the only one having trouble with emotions.

She waited quietly until he was ready to continue. "Parents returned from dinner around 8:15 or 8:30. They were celebrating their wedding anniversary."

A knife thrust of pain cut deep inside Barbara. *Those poor people. They'll never be able to celebrate again.*

Richards flipped a page in his notebook and the rustle of paper focused her thoughts. *Just do the job. Don't think about anything else right now.*

"After calling some friends," he continued, "the parents got worried. The daughter was supposed to come straight home after practice. Fields, the boyfriend, arrived shortly after the parents got here. Says he and the girl were going to watch some TV special at nine."

Richards closed his notebook and stuffed it in his uniform pocket. Barbara thanked him, then returned to the living room. She saw an older version of Mrs. Nelson talking quietly to the distraught mother on the couch.

"The mother's sister," Keith said before she had a chance to ask. "Lives in Dallas."

Barbara watched the two women. It was as if a transfusion of strength had taken place. Aimee's mother sat quietly now, her head cradled in the other woman's arms. It eased Barbara's anguish a notch to see someone who cared that much. God knows the parents would need caring in the days to come.

It was well into the wee hours of the morning before the lab crew finished and the coroner released the body. Barbara felt the weight of total exhaustion when Broyles finally dismissed them. His parting shot did nothing to lift her spirits, "Everyone in my office bright and early."

She drove home slowly, hoping numbness would keep the dreams at bay. All her efforts to achieve detachment weren't working. The victim's faces swam in her mind and her stomach churned.

Maybe it was a desperate grasp at sanity that made her think of Gene. Somewhere deep inside she wished he could be there when she got home. To hold her. To talk to her. To keep the nightmares at bay.

Her practical nature gave her a mental shake. *You're being silly, Barbara Hobkins. You should be well past this stage of falling in love at the drop of a hat.*

"You're right," she said aloud, as if she were actually in a debate. "And who says he'd want to do any of those things, anyway?"

He sat crouched in a corner like a wounded animal, holding his knees and rocking back and forth. He'd done that terrible thing again. *I didn't want to. God! I didn't want to.*

It was cold. He pulled the tattered corner of the quilt tighter against the drafts of night air that found entry in ill-fitting windows. It was always cold here. The only time he didn't feel chilled to the center of his soul was when-

Can't think about that.

If only he could control the raging in his head. If only his hands didn't...

He held one up and squinted at it in the bleak, dusty light. *It's just a hand, isn't it?*

As if some strange apparition had suddenly appeared, he watched, fascinated, as the thick fingers folded one by one.

He dropped the hand quickly. His mother was right. They were evil. She should've cut them off that time. He thought she was going to, but she'd stopped at the last second. And now they were still touching... still doing things they weren't supposed to.

Slamming his fist against the rough plaster on the wall, he felt it go all the way through. Warmth trickled down the back of his hand. He thrust his tongue against the raw knuckle, the mixture of plaster- dust and blood creating an odd, acrid taste. It was not unpleasant, and a familiar sensation warmed his body.

It really wasn't his fault. None of it. It was her fault. Never left him alone. Screaming and yelling all the time. Telling him how stupid and bad he was. How could a man think with some slobbering bitch crowding him into a corner all the time?

He heaved unsteadily to his feet, his fist still in his mouth. The quilt dropped to the bare wooden floor. He had to stop thinking.

Then he remembered the magazine hidden under the mattress. *The pictures would help. They always helped.*

The thin, dirty mattress welcomed his body. He relaxed, the magazine slanted toward the streetlight's pale illumination.

Suddenly, he bolted up. "No! She can't be here." His strident voice bounced off the hollow walls. "It's not fair. This is my place."

He ripped the picture out, crumpled it against his heaving chest, then threw it across the room. The slick ball of paper hung lazily in the air for a moment before falling silently to the floor.

It was starting again. His massive chest released a coarse rattle. His skull pounded, blurring his vision with each heartbeat. *She's like the rest of them. Why won't they leave me alone?*

I can make them.

The thought had a sobering effect. Of course. Why didn't he think of it before? He could cut them out of his life as easily as he'd ripped the picture from the book. It was time to stop playing games.

His shoes squeaked softly as he crossed the room. He bent and picked up the crumpled ball of paper, smoothing it against his hip. His pale eyes narrowed when he looked at the beautiful copper-haired woman. Her green eyes stared back, mocking him.

And he laughed.

I'll show her.

Chapter Ten

Saturday, October 23—Twin Lakes

"This one hangs it," Broyles snarled like a caged lion. "As soon as administration gets wind of it, they'll be all over my ass."

"Maybe we can put a lid on the press," Keith suggested.

Broyles sputtered into his coffee. "Are you nuts? You ever tried to do that? Once they hear about that goddam blanket-"

"It's a quilt, Chief. A random-pattern quilt," Barbara said. "My grandmother had one."

He glared at her, eyes two narrow slits of repressed anger. "I don't give a good goddam what it is. The press is going to run with this like they just heard a starter pistol. The commissioner's been calling every day already. By tomorrow, the mayor will dip his stick into it." Broyles tone turned from sarcasm to anger. "And who do you think's going to take the heat? Me. That's who."

The bluster continued for a full five minutes, while the assembled officers tried to act like it didn't bother then. When the Chief finally wound down, the tension level in the room pulled back from near explosion level. He let his gaze sweep the room, and Barbara wondered if he was daring one of them to make a comment.

Not this officer.

"Who's going to start?" Broyles asked.

Richards spoke up. He was a rookie and didn't know any better. "Nothing's come in from the lab, sir. And the questioning's not-"

"I don't want to hear what we don't have." The veins in Broyles' neck were sticking out again.

Keith cleared his throat. "I think we can rule out the kid as a suspect. His mother alibied him early in the evening. Said he had the phone tied up trying to call the girl. Finally told him to go over there. The rest you know."

The Chief groaned. "Anything else? Anything useful?"

"We're doing the best we can."

"I know." His voice leveled off somewhere between a shout and a roar. "I'm not pointing fingers. Just get off your asses and catch this guy. No time off until we do."

Broyles stormed from the room, closing the door with such force the glass center rattled in its frame.

Keith turned to Barbara with a wry grin. "Always did think he has a way with words."

"But he's right. If we don't get something solid soon, we'll have a full-scale panic on our hands. People are going to connect all the dots. And let's face it, anybody who could brutalize women that way..." Barbara stood and shrugged into her denim jacket, not wanting to think about the details. "He's got to be crazy."

"We don't know it was the same guy." Keith followed her to the door of their office like a puppy on a leash. "Maybe we should keep looking at the girl's boyfriend. The mother never actually saw him between five and seven."

"What do you think? He snuck out between phone calls?" Barbara sat down at her desk and sighed. "But I wish you were right. Two separate murders would be a lot easier to live with than one psycho."

Barbara re-read the preliminary report of the Nelson postmortem. Something in there kept picking away at her subconscious. She scanned it three times before finally realizing what it was. The clothing list didn't include underwear. Could that be a mistake? No. Davies didn't make mistakes.

She pulled the crime-scene report and went through it line by line. No underwear there, either. Barbara grabbed the report and stood, glancing at Keith. "Be right back."

"What's up?"

"Let you know after I talk to Broyles."

Keith watched her leave, letting his bafflement knot his eyebrows. He'd read that report twice. There wasn't anything significant in it. Was there? "Damn her woman's intuition."

Barbara rapped on the Chief's door then pushed it open. "Got a minute?"

Broyles looked up and motioned her in.

"Don't know how important this might be." Barbara pushed a folder out of her way and sat on the small wooden chair across from his desk. "But no underpants were found on the girl's body or at the scene."

"Lots of girls don't wear them now'a days."

"Take it from me, bras may be out but panties are still in, especially where athletics are involved."

He rubbed a finger along the side of his nose, then turned his hand in a 'so what' move.

"Might not be connected. But there's been some trouble at the school. Girl's lockers broken into and panties taken." Barbara leaned back and settled into the narrative now that she had his full attention. "The other day, the principal came in.

Had some panties that had been slashed and returned. Didn't get much from the lab on them. Trace fibers that could connect with a hundred different sources."

"Okay, Hobkins. Get to the point."

"What if the girl *was* wearing underpants that night? And whoever killed her took them?"

The Chief started to protest and Barbara held up a hand. "Just hear me out, okay?"

He nodded.

"My idea is that the murder and the locker room business could be connected. We've got proximity. Similarities." She leaned forward. "And I know this could be stretching it. But maybe the Delgrave murder is tied in, too. The school could be the common denominator."

Instead of calling her nuts, Broyles seemed to consider it all for a moment. "Okay. Let's play with the theory. First, how would he get into the school? Security's as tight as my grandmother's girdle."

"What about an athlete? The boy's locker room is only around the corner. Or maybe a coach? Linen service people? Custodian? Groundskeeper? All those people could get by security."

"As a theory, it's still pretty thin. Hard to connect murder to a prank."

"At least it's an angle. We've been a little short of those so far."

"Don't remind me."

Barbara waited for a moment while he appeared to consider options. "Okay," he finally said. "Work it. See where it leads."

After several hours of tedious investigation, Barbara began to think the thin shred of hope was turning into a dead end. Maybe Keith would do better on checking the school personnel. She'd thought she was on to something when she'd discovered that one of the city employees who worked around the school was the gravedigger they'd talked to at the Delgrave funeral. But his story checked out. Yes, he'd seen the girl. Didn't know who she was, but she was at the track a lot. He'd left that night a little before six, gone straight home for dinner. A story confirmed by his mother.

Then there was the old guy at the nursery with his wry observation, "Ain't no way a body could'a picked up a load of trees at three-thirty, planted 'em by six and still had time to kill someone."

Damn. There has to be something we're missing. Barbara pounded the steering wheel in frustration, then cradled her aching hand in her lap. She was on her way to Gene's on the slim chance he might have seen something. Maybe someone else had planted the trees.

"What a nice surprise," Gene said when he opened the door. He was dressed casually in jeans and a sweatshirt, a small towel tucked in his waistband. He hastily pulled it out. "Can I get you a drink?"

"This isn't a social call," Barbara said as he closed the door behind her. "But I would like to sit down for a minute."

"Rough day?" He removed his briefcase and a newspaper from the couch.

"Lots of 'legwork' as the crime writers like to call it."

"Maybe I could tempt you to stay after the official business is over." He waved toward the kitchen doorway. "Got a pot of spaghetti cooking."

"Wish I could." She sniffed and smiled. "But I've got reports to file."

"You have to eat sometime. And you can leave right after. Won't even make you do dishes."

"You drive a hard bargain. But honestly, I can't."

"Okay. But talk to me while I stir."

Following him into the kitchen, Barbara was struck with how comfortable she felt here with him, so different from the strain last night with Roger. Maybe this was a sign that her decision about him had been right. She was tired of being pulled along like a reluctant colt.

Her mouth watered when she got the full impact of the delicious aroma of basil, oregano, and garlic. What a shame she had to go back and have a cold sandwich with Keith. But she did accept the glass of wine Gene offered.

While he stirred, tested, and played chef, she asked her questions. Unfortunately, all his answers were wrong. He hadn't seen anyone else hanging around the school that night. Yes, the Avery guy was planting the trees. But he didn't see how many the guy had left when he talked to Aimee.

Gene turned from the stove. "How important is this?"

"It's getting less and less, I guess. This morning I was convinced he might be a pretty good suspect. But his story is shoring up."

"He's not one of my favorite people." Gene carried the pasta to the sink and poured it into a steel colander. "But he's been around for a long time. Hard to believe he'd suddenly start killing people."

"I hate to see a good lead go nowhere."

Gene came over and set a steaming plate of spaghetti in front of her.

"I told you-"

"Eat stubborn lady." He topped off her glass of wine. "Didn't someone once say the way to a woman's heart is through her stomach?"

Barbara laughed. "You got your cliché mixed up."

Gene filled another plate and came to sit beside her.

"This is good," she said. "Where'd you ever learn to cook?"

"Sheer necessity." A cloud passed over his face. "Actually I can't take full credit. The recipe was the only good thing my ex-wife left me."

Barbara averted her eyes and concentrated on the food. She knew he'd been married before. He'd mentioned it when they went out the other day but had been short on details. She'd gotten the impression there was a huge wall around the subject with a bold 'hands off' sign and realized it wouldn't do any good to try to chip away at the wall. He'd talk about it when he was ready.

"Didn't mean to spoil the party," Gene said.

"You didn't." She wiped her mouth with a napkin. "I really should leave."

"Sure." He stood and carried their dishes to the sink. "I did promise."

"Are you always a man of your word, Mr. Wilkins?"

Watching the mischief sparkle in her green eyes, Gene fought an overwhelming desire to take her in his arms. *Go slow, man. It's too soon.*

"I try to be, Ms. Hobkins." He purposely matched her bantering tone and was rewarded with a smile.

Reaching for the doorknob, he was startled when the bell rang. He opened the door and saw Tom standing on the porch. Gene started to speak, then saw the newspaper crushed in the other man's grip. Gene exchanged a puzzled glance with Barbara as Tom pushed past him. Then a realization dawned. Tom must have read about Aimee's death.

Striding after his friend, Gene pried the newspaper out of his hand and threw it roughly against the fireplace. Tom just sat there. Oblivious to him. Oblivious to Barbara.

She watched the tableau, which played out almost in slow motion as Gene eased his friend into a chair and hunkered next to him. Tom's movements shouted his internal pain, and Barbara felt anger boil. How terrible it must be to relive the agony of his tragedy through the cold, impersonal account of another victim. No. Not just another victim but a lovely, vivacious young life, brutally crushed just like Susan.

But the dead weren't the only victims of the sickness out there. The living had to go on living with the nightmare day after day.

How long does forgetting take? And how many other lives would be destroyed before it would all be over?

Realizing that her presence was the last thing Tom needed, Barbara motioned to Gene and moved toward the door.

"I feel so stupid," he said. "What can I ever say to him?"

"Maybe nothing. Maybe he doesn't need to hear a thing."

Gene smiled ruefully. "That'll get me off the hook."

Barbara reached up and touched his cheek with the tips of her fingers. Slowly, she traced the smile lines around his mouth as she tried to find something to reassure him. But the moment was way beyond words. Too many emotions crowded her. In a sudden move, she pulled his face to hers and brushed his lips with a kiss. Then she turned and hurried to her car.

After driving for several blocks with the cool evening breeze blowing in her face, she was finally able to think coherently again. One thing was clear. She had to separate her personal life from the case.

On the personal side. She was quickly getting tangled with an unknown entity. Gene was... well, most of all he was a mystery. She knew nothing about him, only how she felt. And the intensity of those feelings scared her. They clouded all reason, making her lead with her heart. Bad move. That's the way it had started with Roger.

Okay. So I'll slow down. Control the emotions and let a little reason come through. That thought brought a smile. Since when had she ever taken her own good advice?

She stopped for a traffic light and drummed her fingers on the steering wheel. Personal life all accounted for. Now, what about the case?

Definitely not any easier to sort out, and she felt a sense of foreboding as she eased the car into gear. She'd promised the families she'd get the killer.

Some promise. She'd just run out of likely suspects.

Maybe I should pray. That thought made her laugh out loud. It had been forever since she'd been on her knees. But right now, appealing to a higher power looked more encouraging than any of her other possibilities.

Chapter Eleven

Monday, October 25—Dallas

Barbara looked around the crowded dining room, trying to find a familiar face. The first time she'd attended the North Dallas Police Association luncheon, she'd been disappointed to find her apprehensions well founded. While the attitudes toward her as a female hadn't been openly hostile, she'd sensed the reserve in most of the officers.

What saved it all was when she sat down next to Steve Harmon, a homicide detective from Dallas Central. While the Chief and even Keith epitomized the typical male police officer, Harmon, for all his twenty years on the job, was an antithesis. He was slight of build, with a great mop of unruly black hair sprinkled liberally with gray. Soft spoken, he had a quick mind and a natural instinct.

He'd admitted to her that he had to answer to his partner, Brady, for his reliance on intuition as much as Barbara answered to Keith. Perhaps that affinity drew them together more than anything else. Harmon was the big brother that Barbara never had, and she'd relied on his judgment a great deal in the past four years. This afternoon, she looked forward to running her current case by a fresh eye and an objective viewpoint.

She spotted Steve at a table toward the back and threaded her way toward him.

"Missed you last month," Harmon said. "Yours is usually the prettiest face here."

"Sorry I let you down." Barbara hung her sweater over the back of a chair, eased the strap of her shoulder holster where it dug into her collarbone, and sat down. "Had a bug. Spent the afternoon wishing I'd just die and get it over with."

"That's what's great about Texas in the fall. Never know what new virus will blow in with the latest weather change."

Barbara looked around the room and spotted another friendly face. Sarah Kingsly, who also worked at Dallas Central. She returned her wave then turned back. "We could always go to Iceland. Weather's pretty stable over there."

Harmon laughed. "But they don't have Margaritas." He held up his glass. "Want one?"

"If I did, I'd pass out."

He regarded her with thoughtful brown eyes. "Rough going?"

"You hear we had another one?"

He nodded.

"Right now I think I'm just mad. Madder 'n hell that whoever did it is still running around."

"You'll get him."

"I wonder..." Barbara let the sentence trail off as the waiter served them each a plate of steaming enchiladas. A local restaurant always catered lunch. This month is was Julio's.

Dr. Davies was the featured speaker this afternoon but Barbara didn't catch most of what he said. It was hard enough trying to follow the strange paths his mind took in a one-on-one conversation, but with the background noise of a hundred or so people eating lunch, it was impossible.

She slowly ate bites of the gooey cheese and beef mixture and thought about the functions of these meetings. Officers from a number of departments gathered regularly to trade information and sometimes pick up a lead. She remembered the case Harmon reviewed in August, a Jane Doe homicide.

The body'd been found in a lake, and Barbara had commiserated with him on the lack of leads. His comment, "Sometimes I wonder if our job isn't measured in defeat," seemed as appropriate for her case today.

After Davies stepped down from the microphone, Harmon pushed his empty plate away and stuck a toothpick in his mouth.

"How's your Jane Doe case?" Barbara asked.

"Pending. It feels like a time bomb. Just sitting there ticking away."

"What makes it so different from any other?"

"I don't know." He paused to roll the toothpick from one side of his mouth to the other. "I've got a feeling. You know. One of our infamous 'feelings.'"

Barbara laughed. "When was the last time you were told to stuff it?"

"This morning." He smiled. "But back to the Jane Doe. Remember I told you how bad the body looked? Been in the water for several weeks. Eaten by fish and God knows what."

Barbara regarded the cold, greasy enchilada sauce congealed around the edges of her plate and waved him to silence. "Have a heart."

Harmon tilted his chair back on two legs, smiled, and continued. "The full medical report indicated the body was mutilated before it was put in the water."

"How could they determine that?"

"It was our illustrious Dr. Davies who first came up with it. Fish feed by biting and tearing at their prey. Most of what happened to this body fit that pattern. But Davies found some things out of the ordinary. Including a fracture in the neck cartilage. And bone bruises. It would've taken a hell of a big fish to do that."

Barbara found the fracture of the cartilage interesting. Same thing as Delgrave and Nelson. Did she dare hope? "You see anything that could connect to our cases?"

"Other than cause of death, nothing. The MO doesn't fit. And why the hell would some guy kill a woman in Dallas then two in Twin Lakes? And the fact that my Jane Doe is still unclaimed makes me think she was one of the lost and forgotten. You know, homeless. Or a hooker. What would she have in common with yours?"

"I don't know." Barbara shrugged. "But what the hell. It wouldn't hurt to look. We're not getting anywhere on our own."

"You're welcome to my files." Harmon finished off his drink and set the glass down. "But unless something else comes up, I don't know what good it'll do." He smiled. "Your guy didn't use yellow rope, did he?"

"No. But we're both looking for a very disturbed personality. Maybe he forgot his rope this time."

Her fatigue and disappointment felt like a boulder as Barbara left the luncheon. She'd attended with a vague hope of... *Of what?* That she or Harmon might get this great flash of enlightenment that would solve both the cases? She really didn't know.

As if to insure her depression, low, gray clouds gave way to rain, and she realized it had dropped ten degrees in the past hour.

"Makes my day," she said and dashed across the glistening parking lot to her car.

She dabbed at the faint mascara smudges under her eyes, several raindrops still held captive in her upper lashes. She smiled at her reflection in the rearview mirror. Cover girls could swim, shower, jog, and God knows what without a smear. *How come they get so lucky?*

The desire to go home to a hot bath tugged at her. It would be nice to just walk away. Call Marcy. See a movie. Anything to take her mind off the drudgery ahead. She didn't look forward to running in and out of the rain, which was obviously settling in for a long visit, to keep appointments she didn't want to make in the first place.

She had to talk to the Nelsons again. And a couple of Aimee's school friends.

The emotional detachment she usually cushioned herself with, just wasn't there this time. *But let's face it, girl. You never felt so close.*

She'd wanted to discuss this with Harmon, but a last minute attack of embarrassment won out. Would he laugh at her thought that her apartment break-in could be connected to the cases? Murder and mischief? The link seemed ridiculous.

The steady spatter of the rain against the car calmed her jangled thoughts.. She watched small rivulets of water form slowly at the top of the windshield, gain speed, then suddenly get sucked into a final tributary.

Even as a child, she'd liked the finality of rain. It was so definite and fit the rest of her life so well. She could recall very few 'maybes' in her childhood. Her parents were strong and steady, and she'd grown up determined and confident. 'Maybes' wasted time, gave no direction. A 'maybe' was gray, and her orderly structure demanded black and white.

A familiar feeling of confidence replaced the doubt. She cracked the car window, took a couple of deep breaths, and pulled into traffic. *One day at a time. One thing at a time.*

He quietly closed the door and stood for a moment to let his eyes adjust to the darkness. He wouldn't turn on lights. Last time they'd almost given him away. But not this time. This time he wasn't going to do anything stupid. He'd waited too long for her to leave to screw up now.

It must have been an hour at least that he'd crouched under the hedge watching the apartment. Skeletal bushes afforded little protection from the slow, steady drizzle, and now his clothes clung soddenly to his body. But it was worth it to be here now.

She thinks she's so fuckin' smart. I'll show her. He moved down the long hall, pulling a small package from beneath his nylon Windbreaker. *I bet she doesn't even know I took them.*

He remembered the other time. He hadn't planned for anything to happen. Only wanted to be there. To see where she lived. But once in her bedroom, he hadn't been able to control himself. The rumpled bed and all those flimsy silk things flung casually around the room, took control. He'd picked up a pale, blue nightgown and crushed it to his face. It felt so good. And it smelled so sweet.

Remembering brought tiny beads of sweat to his forehead. His breath rattled harshly in a dry throat. It was happening all over again. He watched himself as the scene came alive in his mind...

...The feel of slick, soft, silk against his face. The throb of his heart, pounding faster and faster, like a pacemaker gone berserk. The sudden warm rush of blood through his veins, an urgent sensation his body responded to involuntarily.

Then the panties at his feet. A bright splash of red against the pale carpet. His pulse quickens even more. His head rolls back and forth. He has no control. His hands take over, caressing the panties and smothering his face in the sweet, pungent smell of her.

The hands work fervently. He can't stop. He's gone too far already. His mind rages as his body seeks complete satisfaction. Why does it have to be this way? Why do they have this power over him?

Then the heat of passion dwindles and his mind slowly returns to reality. He looks at his hands, those extensions of the horror that lived in clouded corners of his mind. They won again. Now he hasthat terrible mess to clean up. It isn't his fault. He doesn't want to do it...

Pulling back to the present, he vowed he wouldn't do that again. Wouldn't go into her bedroom this time. *Too dangerous. She'd know this time for sure.*

He stopped for a moment, puzzled. Didn't he want her to know? *Of course. That's what it's all about.*

Smiling, he turned the knob on the bedroom door and heard the soft click as it opened.

An inner alarm went off the minute Barbara stepped inside the apartment. Charlotte was absent again. She slid her Walther P-38 out of her shoulder holster and tried to swallow her pounding heart. Weapon held to her side, she moved cautiously down the hall and slipped into the dark living room. She'd forgotten to leave the table lamp on again. Or had she?

Trembling fingers turned the switch. The sudden click shattered the stillness and made her jump. She looked around. No Charlotte. Nothing disturbed. The kitchen proved to be empty, too, but the cat dish was still full of this morning's seafood platter.

All the fear she'd tried to push aside since the last time swelled to the brink of overflowing. Her instinct was to turn and run. But the professional took over. *This is just like any other break-in you've investigated. You can do it.*

Strengthened by the pep talk, Barbara walked quietly down the hall and gently pushed on the bedroom door. The scrape of resistance between the bottom of the door and the thick pile of carpet sounded absurdly loud. She held her weapon in front of her then eased around the doorframe. Careful not to present a target, she paused and let her eyes adjust. Nothing unusual lurked in the shadows, so she reached across her chest to flick the light switch with her left hand.

The room was empty and a sigh slipped through her lips. But the relief wavered as her eyes were drawn to the bed. There, neatly on top of her gown, was a small package loosely wrapped in wrinkled brown paper and tied with a tattered white string.

Proof. Undeniable proof that someone had been there slapped Barbara across the face. Fear and anger pumped her heart faster.

Carefully, she touched the bundle with the barrel of the revolver. She strained her ears for any sound of ticking and strained her eyes for wires. Finally convinced the package didn't contain an explosive, she picked it up by the string. A gentle pull opened the bundle, spilling a pair of underwear to the floor. Confused, Barbara again used the gun barrel to pick up the underwear.

Horror filled her eyes as she realized the panties were hers. Marcy had given her the red-initialed bikinis with the assertion that every woman needed a touch of scarlet in her life. There was no mistake. This was Barbara's touch of scarlet.

Charlotte poked her head out from under the bed, her cold nose touching Barbara's leg, and she almost fainted. She bent down and picked up the cat, finding comfort in the warm, sandy tongue on her cheek. *What the hell is going on here?*

With an effort, Barbara forced herself back to the role of the objective observer and looked at the package again. There was another pair of panties inside. Not hers.

Fighting a surge of panic, she dialed the station.

The nightmare came flooding back. Susan Delgrave, Aimee Nelson, and now this shadow of her vulnerability.

On impulse, she picked up the phone for one more call, then put Charlotte in the sanctuary of her crate. The apartment was about to be invaded by more strange men than the poor cat could probably stand.

Gene arrived on the heels of Broyles and Reeves. His protective move to Barbara's side caused the Chief to look at him with interest. But any thoughts he had, he kept to himself.

"You all right?" Gene asked, touching her arm in an awkward gesture.

"Yes. I made sure nobody was lurking."

Gene shot Broyles a murderous look, which would have disarmed a lesser man.

The Chief had to stifle a smile. What did Wilkins expect? Of course Barbara would search the apartment. This guy's chivalry might get shoved up his ass if he didn't watch it.

"Okay, Hobkins," Broyles said. "Let's go over it from the top."

Barbara sat down on the sofa, Gene beside her. "It was just like last time-"

"What do you mean, 'last time?'" Gene was on his feet. "You didn't tell me about any last time."

Broyles saw where this could go in a hurry, so he held up a hand to Gene, then nodded to Barbara. "Go on."

While Keith moved around in the background, dusting for prints, she related her actions from the time she'd arrived home. Broyles was glad she was a trained officer. Her account was a relief from the scattered statements he usually got.

"I found this after I called." Barbara pushed a torn wrinkled page from a magazine across the table to the Chief.

The face that laughed up at him so closely resembled Barbara, Broyles choked. His eyes were caught by the message left in vivid red letters scrawled across the page:

...A MOUSE KILLED A CAT...BUT FIRST...HE PLAYED

The silence was deafening, then Broyles slammed a hand on the table. "I'm posting a guard."

"No. She's coming home with me." Gene put a protective arm around Barbara.

"Gene!" She glanced at Broyles then back to Gene.

"I mean it." His jaw was rigid.

"We take care of our own," Broyles said.

"Just a minute." Barbara jerked roughly out of Gene's hold and stood. "Contrary to popular belief, I can take care of myself."

"We can't ignore this." Broyles gestured to the picture.

"I'm not. Just keeping it in perspective." She glared at him. "How many threats have you gotten in your career?"

He shifted. "A few."

"Did you call out the SWAT team?"

"Don't be absurd, Hobkins. There's a danger in taking this too lightly."

"I'm not." She leaned over and picked up the picture. "I respect this. And I'll be careful. I'd even appreciate an extra patrol now and then. But I refuse to be intimidated." Now she swept them both with blazing eyes. "You want to play King Arthur, find yourselves another maiden."

Keith stepped out of the bedroom just in time to catch her last remark, and he burst out laughing.

Barbara whirled. "What's so funny?"

He smothered the sound. "Nothing. Nothing at all."

"Good. I'm going to make coffee." She stormed from the room.

"I'll be damned," Broyles said.

"What did we do?" Gene asked.

Broyles shrugged. "She gets riled about this equality thing. But this is the worst I've seen."

"Maybe it's the shock of tonight," Keith offered, then motioned to Gene. "Go see if she's okay. We'll finish out here."

With the sharp clanging of pans giving him pause, Gene took a hesitant step into the kitchen. "Truce," he said softly. "Didn't mean to offend."

Barbara turned, and he was surprised to see tears glistening in her eyes. She took a hiccuping breath. "I'm not a poor old grandmother who needs looking after."

"Of course not." He closed the distance and put an arm around her. "Maybe I did overreact a bit. But believe me, it wasn't because you're a woman. I'd say the same things to Tom."

His tenderness touched her sensitive spot, making it hard to stem the flood of warm tears that spilled out of her eyes. All the shock and anxiety came out while Gene held her tight. Neither of them heard the discreet cough in the doorway.

Broyles stepped back with a foolish grin. Apparently, his favorite woman detective had found a man. It was about time she was rid of that arrogant cowboy.

Deciding on another tact, the Chief called out in a loud voice," Hold the coffee. We're going to take this stuff in and call it a night."

Barbara stepped into the doorway with a flush on her cheeks. "You sure, Chief? It's almost done."

"It's late." He started to give her a sermon about keeping her doors locked, then changed his mind. It might start another tirade. "I'll arrange the patrols," he said. "You take care."

Gene left a short time later. Unlike the Chief, he chose to give the sermon. His concern was a little too close to Roger's for her comfort, but she was too tired to argue.

Once alone, the uncertainty started again. After the intensity of the feelings she'd shared with Gene in the kitchen, his hasty departure was a bit disconcerting. If he was so worried about her, why did he leave almost on the heels of the detectives?

She went back to the kitchen and looked at the fresh pot of coffee. Why not? She wasn't about to sleep tonight anyway. Despite her assurance to the men that she could take care of herself, she felt very alone and vulnerable.

Going to the door to check the lock for the third time, she realized she had to turn her mind to something else, or go crazy. She sat on a stool at the kitchen counter and pulled the message pad over. She wrote one word: PANTIES and put a question mark after it.

Was there a connection between the business at the school, her apartment, and the murder of Aimee Nelson? Did the extra pair she found here tonight belong to the girl? Would the killer really have had the balls to leave them?

Barbara tapped the pencil against her cheek and considered the questions. They seemed almost too bizarre to be even asked, but what if she was on a track here?

Aimee's mother had assured Barbara that the girl always wore underwear. Therefore, the killer must have taken her panties with him.

Letting her mind free-associate with all the possibilities, she quickly jotted questions that might have answers. And questions that still needed them.

Chapter Twelve

Tuesday, October 26—Twin Lakes

Royce Wertco barely glanced at the paper as he passed the newsstand, but the headline caught his eye, "No Leads in Brutal Slaying of Co-ed."

He fished change from the pocket of his low-slung jeans and bought a paper. He knew how to get one for nothing. In fact, he knew how to get all the money from the box. But he figured, what the hell? He still had plenty of money from painting old Barnett's house. Besides, it was too risky doing it in broad daylight in the middle of a mall. One thing Royce didn't need was another run-in with the police. Not when he was so close to his eighteenth birthday and his ticket out.

Unfolding the paper, he sat on a nearby bench. This was the first time he'd bothered to read about the murder since the news came out Saturday morning. He mentally sounded the words out. 'A department spokesperson told reporters today that there are no leads in the apparent homicide of sixteen-year-old Aimee Nelson, a former student at Twin Lakes High. Nelson, the second apparent homicide victim in the past month, was found late Friday evening. The coroner determined time-of-death to be between four and six PM.'

Geez. I thought it happened Saturday morning.

Royce skimmed the rest of the article, which included a fairly graphic account of her injuries, then set the paper aside.

Thinking about Aimee being attacked like that, his first reaction was, *'What a crying shame someone so luscious had been taken out that way.'* He'd been trying for two months to get a date with her. In fact, he'd talked to her just the other day on the front steps of the school.

She'd been firm in her refusals all along. Said she already had a boyfriend. But he'd never let a little fact like that stand in his way before. So he'd persisted, and that day their conversation got heated. A crowd gathered, drawn by the loud voices. *God! That was Friday. Just a few hours before she was killed.*

When the full significance of that fact hit him, Royce felt the first flutters of panic stir his bowels. *Son of a bitch! The fuckin' cops are gonna be all over me.*

That wasn't just idle speculation. Royce had been pulled in enough over past years to write a book on police procedure. That history would be as incriminating as the connection he had to the dead girl.

Why had he been stupid enough to go by her house after the fight at school? Sure as shittin' some busybody had probably been looking out her window just as he'd started up Aimee's front walk.

Now the panic pounded in his temples, making it hard to think. And the sweat trickling down his sides was from more than just the late afternoon sun slanting through the plate-glass window behind him.

Goddam. They found her body practically on the doorstep of that old shed. Haven't been there for months. But how long do prints last? *Shit! What kind of mess am I in now?*

His hands trembled so badly he couldn't pick up the paper. He looked around quickly, afraid the police might already be on the way.

Forcing some welcome air into his deflated lungs, he stood and walked as calmly as he could out of the shopping center. He felt exposed every inch of the way.

He'd go home and contact some of his friends. They'd know how to help. He wasn't supposed to talk to them since his parole. *But, what the hell? Parole violation ain't nothin' to what they'll hang on me if I don't get the hell out of here. And fast.*

Intent on his fear, Royce didn't notice the car parked across from his house until it was too late. When he did, he recognized the two men in the front seat. Juvenile officers.

He willed his shaky legs not to carry him off in a blind panic.

"Hello, Royce." Detective Cromwell pulled his long, lanky frame out of the car as Royce drew near. "Where've you been?"

The officer's partner stayed in the car, and Royce shot a nervous look from one to the other. "Hey, Man. I'm clean. You got no call hasslin' me."

"Take it easy." Cromwell gave him a lazy smile, the flash of white softening the hard planes of his dark face. Maybe it was supposed to be reassuring, but it did nothing to calm Royce's mounting fear. He'd seen that smile too many times before.

"Just want to ask you a few questions," Cromwell continued in a conversational tone. "Nothing to get in a lather about."

'Just two guys talking on the street.' Royce knew that was the impression the cop wanted him to have. But he knew better. He licked his lips and swallowed against the feeling of impending doom churning in his stomach. "I ain't done nothing," he said, a shade too loud.

The flicker of interest that crossed the officer's face wasn't reassuring. Royce felt the blood drain from his head. *Shit! I've done it now.*

Royce knew he was right when Cromwell lost the 'good 'ol boy' demeanor and hit him with the first question. "Where were you last Friday from four until six-thirty?"

"Around."

"Around where?"

Intense dark eyes seemed to look clear through to his soul and Royce shifted slightly. "I dunno. Just around. Had to see a guy about a job."

"What time?"

"About seven."

"What about before?"

"Listen!" Royce tensed, knowing he was on the losing end of this. "I don't have to-"

Cromwell's voice cut in like a cold edge of steel. "You'll do exactly as I say."

Suddenly Royce bolted. He couldn't just stand there, knowing he didn't have the right answers. Darting between the houses, he dashed for the back fence like a racer heading for the finish line. Once over that, he might have a chance in the maze of streets and back alleys he knew so well. It was his only hope.

The officer was quicker than Royce thought he could be. Just as he frantically scratched at the top of the wood fence, Cromwell grabbed his leg and pulled him roughly to the ground. Face pushed in the dank earth, Royce felt the cold weight of cuffs snare him like a rabbit in a trap.

"Call headquarters," Cromwell told his partner who arrived huffing and puffing. "We got a suspect in the Nelson murder."

"No way, man!" Royce fought to break the officer's grip. "You ain't pinning that on me."

Cromwell ignored the outburst and proceeded to read the kid his rights.

A tingle of apprehension raised the hairs on Barbara's arms as she unlocked her apartment. If she saw any signs of an uninvited guest again, she was definitely moving.

Exhaustion had drained her inner well of strength. At times she felt like a time bomb was ticking away in her gut, and her nerves were attuned to that last little click that preceded an explosion. It was becoming increasingly difficult not to see menacing strangers lurking in every shadow.

That's why she'd decided to take a break and come home for lunch. Maybe she and the cat needed a little oasis of normalcy.

As the door opened, Barbara saw Charlotte's furry form bounce down the hall. It was the most beautiful sight she could imagine, and she bent down to pick up the cat. She carried her into the living room, debating about what to have for lunch. *Should it be something frozen, or the tin can standby?*

The morning had been an exercise in futility. Aimee's mother wasn't able to say for sure if the panties belonged to her daughter or not. The girl had done her own laundry for some time now. And used her babysitting money to buy some of her own clothes.

Barbara remembered how the woman's voice broke over the explanation that it was all part of Aimee starting to exert some independence. "My baby was growing-" The rest was lost in tears.

Maybe there's something to be said for celibacy after all.

Don't do this. Time enough to sort out your life after you sort out the case.

She sat heavily on the couch and slipped off her shoes. "What do you think, cat? Should we live it up and have frozen shrimp or-"

The shrill ring of the phone cut her off. Charlotte bounded to the floor as Barbara reached for the receiver. "Hello?"

"This is a recall notice." Keith's voice battled for dominance over the interference on the line. "Cromwell brought us a present a few minutes ago."

"What?"

"A suspect. Chief wants us both at the station, STAT."

"On my way." She slammed the receiver down and grabbed her purse on the run. *Finally, something positive.*

Barbara observed the interrogation through a one-way glass. Watching Royce squirm in a hard chair, with the chief towering over him, brought back vivid pictures of the kid she'd busted three years ago. *If only he'd stayed scared.*

The door opened, and she turned from the window. "Hey, Keith."

"Vaughn's bringing the mother in. Chief wants you to talk to her." Keith nodded toward the scene in the other room. "What a break, huh?"

"Let's not file the case tonight, okay?"

"I didn't mean..." His smile faded. "What's bugging you?"

Barbara turned back to the window and watched Royce swipe a trembling hand through his dirty blonde hair. "Look at him. Does he look like a cold-blooded killer?"

"Nobody looks the part, Hobkins. Remember Jack the Ripper?"

"Yeah. He was a madman. And so was whoever did our two women. Not some misguided kid."

"How quickly you forget Columbine."

"This is different."

Whatever Keith was going to say was lost when Vaughn poked his head in the door. "Hobkins? We got the old lady. Where do you want her?"

"My office. Be right there."

As she walked down the hall to grab a cup of coffee, Barbara tried to cast Royce in the role of the killer. He failed her audition. She couldn't believe he'd crossed over that fine line into madness. No amount of circumstantial evidence would convince her of that. And Keith's comment was a low blow. This was nothing like the craziness that prompted kids to take guns to school and play Rambo to some misguided slight.

Barbara paused outside her office and looked at Mrs. Wertco. The woman sagged in the visitor's chair like someone had pulled a plug in her feet and all her insides had drained out.. Mousy brown hair clung to her head in a tight perm, and her shoulders slumped beneath a frayed black sweater. The woman turned startled blue eyes toward her as Barbara entered the room, then she started to rise. "Miss Hobkins... it isn't true. Tell me it isn't."

Touching the woman's shoulder, Barbara eased her back to the chair. "It's okay."

"But... that officer told me... you don't really think my Royce..." Her voice broke and she dabbed at her eyes with a rumpled tissue.

"We're just questioning him. No charges have been filed." Barbara was glad she'd taken a few minutes to compose herself before facing the woman. She sat down and opened her notebook. "Now, let's see if you can help him."

Unfortunately, a desire to help wasn't enough. Mrs. Wertco had no idea what Royce had been doing on the afternoon of the Nelson murder. In fact, she hadn't seen him since Friday morning.

But, yes, Royce knew the Nelson girl. "I think he was trying to get a date with her."

"What makes you think that?"

"I heard him one day on the phone. He was sort'a mad. Yelled a little."

"How do you know he was talking to her?"

"He said, 'you think you're too good for me, Aimee Nelson. We'll see about that.'"

"Are you sure that's what he said?"

"Just because he argued with her don't mean he hurt her." The woman beseeched Barbara with tear-stained eyes. "You know my boy. You believed in him before."

Barbara sighed. *Belief isn't enough. I need cold, hard facts.*

Latching on to one small hope, Barbara pulled the picture of the quilt out of the Nelson file and showed it to Mrs. Wertco. The presence of the quilt at the murder scene still had to be explained. If they couldn't connect Royce to it, maybe it would cast doubts in other official minds.

The older woman studied the picture for a full minute after Barbara asked if she recognized the quilt. "I think so," she finally said. "It looks like one I used to have."

"Know where it is now?"

Mrs. Wertco shrugged. "Royce was always takin' old blankets and things. To the lake or out to some old building where he met friends. Said it was cold and drafty.

Barbara tapped the picture with her finger. "Is this yours?"

"I'm... I'm not sure."

"Surely you'd recognize your own quilt."

"I'm sorry." Tears welled in eyes already ravaged. "It wasn't mine... I mean, I didn't make it. It was a gift. And...well, I never did pay much attention. To the design, I mean. Guess this could be it."

Barbara wondered if the poor woman knew how much deeper she was digging the hole for Royce. She looked at the face across from her. It was puffy and splotched red with tears, the silent appeal strong. Barbara broke eye contact. *Damn it. I can't do anything. Why the hell didn't he go straight when he had the chance? Why did he run from Cromwell?*

Barbara couldn't ask the mother these questions, and she wasn't even sure she could ask the kid. His cooperation had been minimal even the first time, almost like he hadn't really given a damn.

She remembered some of his behavior. Cocky. Almost mocking her and the system. And that one incident outside the courthouse. The memory flashed through her mind...

...Standing in the glaring sunlight on the cracked cement steps. The mill of attorneys and spectators. Then an odd crunching sound.

She turns, almost collides with Royce. He's staring intently at his feet. Her eyes follow. He stands on his left foot, the right hovering several inches above one of the many crickets littering the steps.

Inch by inch he lowers his foot, slowly crushing the insect. Black and yellow goo dots the step.

She looks at him, and he returns her gaze with a lazy smile. Then he lowers his eyes and holds them to a spot below her waist, savagely scrapping his foot across the matted ooze. Then he walks away...

Recalling the image made Barbara shudder. Had she misjudged him? Could he have killed Aimee Nelson? Did he squash her life with the same sadistic abandonment he'd used on insects?

"Miss Hobkins?" The fragile voice snapped Barbara out of her thoughts. "Is that all?"

"For now. If we need anything else, we'll call."

"What about my boy? Can I see him?"

Barbara averted her eyes. "It'll be a while. Why don't you go back home? Someone will notify you about visiting."

With Mrs. Wertco gone, Barbara sat back and absently doodled on the margin of her notebook. Things looked bad for the kid. If his mother was right, the dead girl had rejected him. And the fact that the quilt found with the body could belong to Mrs. Wertco did little to improve his situation.

"Just finished talking with the Chief." Keith burst into the room, high on excitement. "Royce admitted knowing the girl. And get this." He put his large hands on the desk and leaned toward Barbara. "He said he had a fight with her Friday afternoon."

He paused, maybe waiting for her to get caught up in the excitement. But her heart wasn't in it.

"There's more," he said. "Broyles is taking Wertco before the magistrate right now. He wants us to get in gear and build the case."

Barbara's numb silence failed to register on Keith. "But not tonight." He straightened. "He said to get on it first thing in the morning. Except for your interview with the mother. Wants that report on his desk tonight."

Barbara felt the numbness give way to frustration. "That's just great," she snapped. "What good will that-" She stopped and shrugged.

"We only have seventy-two hours." Keith rummaged through his pockets for a breath mint. "Either we file charges or let him go."

"I know that. Now get out so I can finish the report. I want to go home."

His eyelids drooped, and every few seconds his chin bounced off his chest. Then he'd jerk awake. Wouldn't do to fall asleep. That patrol car might come back. *What was it? An hour ago it had come by?* Lucky he'd seen it in time to drive around the block. But the longer he stayed, the more his nerves jumped. He might not see the patrol next time.

Where the hell is she? It had been such a perfect setup. Then just when he was starting toward the door, she'd burst out and ran to her car. He'd quickly turned away. He was sure she hadn't seen him. But why wasn't she back yet? *Three fucking hours!*

Maybe she didn't just go off for a good time like he first thought. It didn't take that long to rip off a little piece.

A warm flush of desire spread through him as he pictured her firm, young body at his command. He could show her what it's like to be with a real man. Mentally, he toyed with the idea until it created an urgency that threatened to consume him.

Stop it you asshole. That's the kind of thinkin' that always starts trouble. Stick to the plan. It's gotta be quick with her. She's not like the others, too stupid to know until it's too late. She's smart. Gotta make the move. Then after... well, after will take care of itself.

Impatient, he checked his watch. Twelve-thirty and still no sign of her. Frustration simmered deep inside. Why'd she have to ruin his plan? Did she know? Was she playing a game of her own?

From the beginning, there'd been something about her: a something reflected in those green eyes that told him his time was almost up. He'd lived with that warning growing stronger while his obsession clung like a fat parasite.

If she hadn't gone running off, it would be over now. He wouldn't have to worry about her anymore.

Suddenly his thoughts froze. *What if it's already too late? What if she beat me? Found something?*

He considered the possibility. Maybe the last one had been a mistake. He'd never done one so close before. But he'd been careful. Done it just like the other. No way they'd know the difference. And that other part of his life? He'd always kept that separate. No one could know.

But still. Maybe this was a warning. Maybe he should forget about this one. But even as the thought entered his mind, he knew he could never just forget. The bitch haunted him. Made him crazy. He had to get rid of her.

Not tonight, though. Another time. Another place.

Chapter Thirteen

Tuesday, October 26—Twin Lakes

Half asleep, Barbara banged on her alarm clock to stop the horrible clang of noise. It couldn't be time to get up. But, as the fog clogging her brain cleared and the ringing continued, she realized it was the telephone. She reached over and grabbed the receiver, expecting to hear Keith tell her she was late for duty assignments.

Gene's voice surprised her. "Just heard the morning news," he said. "Royce Wertco. Who'd've thought?"

"Yeah." Barbara ran a hand across her face in an effort to fully wake up.

"You okay?"

"Hang on a sec 'til I get some coffee." She laid the receiver down, then dragged her body into the kitchen. Setting the kettle on the stove to boil, she reached for a mug and her jar of instant coffee. Then she quickly splashed her face with cold water from the tap before picking up the extension. "Thanks. Now I feel almost human."

"No problem. Guess you had a late night?"

"Didn't end until after two this morning." Barbara poured hot water in the mug and stirred. "Interviews. Reports."

"I'm having a hard time getting my mind around the idea of this kid being a killer."

His words echoed her sentiments so closely that Barbara wished she could share her doubts with him. But that was out of the realm of professionalism. Instead of responding, she took the first welcome swallow of coffee.

"Do you think..." Gene seemed to be having some trouble putting words to his question. "Could he have been involved with Susan's death?"

"We can't say."

"It might be a help to Tom. To know for sure."

"I know." Barbara rested a hip against the edge of the counter. "Wish I could be more definite. But we just have to wait and see what kind of evidence turns up."

"Anything I can do?"

"We'll need to talk to the teachers who had contact with Royce. Students too. It would help for you to pave the way. Talk to the kids. You know how they can be with their wild stories. We want as little of that as possible."

"I'll do what I can."

"Thanks." Barbara hung up and headed toward the shower. She had lots of things to do, people to see, and she damn well needed to wake up.

Late afternoon sun fought its way through layers of grime on a small window in the west squad room of the TLPD. Barbara wondered how long ago the glass had been cleaned. It looked like centuries of dust, smoke, and heating oil had accumulated. But the assembled officers weren't there to rate the cleanliness of the place. It was time to see what they had on Royce Wertco. Reports had come filtering in all day from officers taking statements, and the evidence was stacking up fast.

Shortly before lunch, Barbara had questioned the Nelson's again. The distraught couple knew nothing of Wertco or his association with their daughter. The only boy they knew about was Tony.

Barbara's heart had gone out to Mr. Nelson. A shell of human agony, he'd sat unmoving, as silent tears streaked his face before stopping abruptly in a gray stubble of beard. The killer had left one victim to be buried and two more to slowly bury themselves one shovel-full of grief at a time.

After her painful encounter with the parents, Barbara had met Keith for a quick lunch at Grande Tacos. Over three of his favorite burritos, he'd dismissed her reservations about Wertco. Her psycho theory, according to Keith, was the result of way too many 'head' classes.

Now she sat in the crowded squad room, still wondering if they were all going down the wrong path. Psychology courses or not, Barbara couldn't cast the kid as the killer. Not yet. Despite the mounting evidence, she didn't buy it. She held firm to the belief that Aimee Nelson and Susan Delgrave shared a common killer. In Barbara's mind, someone Wertco's age could not have accumulated the rage unleashed on both women. Not without some definitive signs in his past. There were none. No abuse. No questionable disappearances of pets. No brushes with the law until three years ago. Not the stuff serial killers are made of. If she were going to type the killer, it would be someone like the gravedigger, someone with more than fear in his eyes.

"This just came in from Crosby," Chief Broyles' booming voice brought Barbara to full alert.

"Statement from a Christine Petner, who, in her own words, was 'Aimee's best friend.' This girl's afraid of Wertco. Told Crosby she even warned Aimee to be careful of him."

Broyles caught the shadow passing over Barbara's face. "Hobkins," he said loudly. "Whose side are you on?"

She was saved from having to answer when Keith burst into the room. He waved a large manila folder. "Just got this from forensic," he said with a triumphant expression. "And guess what?" He directed the question to Broyles.

"This isn't a goddam quiz show."

The Chief's cutting remark only slightly dampened Keith's excitement. "We've got prints from that old shed at the Nelson crime scene. A perfect match with our own Royce Wertco."

A wide grin spread across Broyles' face. "Now we're getting somewhere."

"What about the first murder?" Barbara asked, deliberately avoiding Keith's eyes.

"If we can tie him to it, fine. Otherwise, we go with the premise of two separate killers." Broyles tugged at the knot in his tie and continued as if lecturing a student body. "Wertco may have followed the Delgrave MO to divert suspicion. According to the medical reports, the mutilations were similar. Not identical. The woman could've been killed by a drifter who's since moved on."

The logical side of Barbara admitted that it was a damn good theory, but she still had a gut hunch they were cheering too soon. But, as a current of excitement ran through the room, she decided now was not the time to voice those doubts.

On the way out to the hallway, Keith tapped her on the shoulder. "Got a minute?"

She paused and moved away from the door. "What's up?"

Keith shuffled and watched a bug crawl along the baseboard. "Um... sorry about spouting off last night."

"That's okay. If you didn't argue with me now and then I wouldn't know when I'm right."

Chapter Fourteen

Wednesday, October 27—Twin Lakes

After morning duty assignments, Barbara returned to her office alone. Keith was going out on a new case. Wishing she'd brought a cup of coffee, she sorted the pile of mail on her desk. Pamphlets, credit card applications and... Carefully, she picked up the envelope. It was addressed to her in a nearly illegible scrawl, resembling a child's first attempt at cursive.

A vivid picture of the crude message left in her apartment flashed through her mind. *Oh, God. Not again.* She stared at the envelope, then sighed. *Only one way to find out. Open it.*

The envelope was too small and too light to contain an explosive, so part of her mind told her it was safe. She slit the edge with her fingernail file and used tweezers to pull out a piece of paper. Plain, white bond with the words YOU ARE WRONG printed in rough block letters.

Another crank? Or someone with first-hand knowledge? Only the real killer knew for sure Wertco was innocent.

With mounting excitement, she took the envelope and message to Broyles' office. Still holding the paper in tweezers, she handed it to the Chief.

He scanned the message, looked at her then sighed. "This could be nothing. Just one of those weirdoes who crawl out to share the limelight of a high profile case."

"What if it isn't? What if it's the killer trying to tell us something?"

"Christ, Hobkins. That sounds like a line in a B movie."

"So we ignore it?" She motioned to the note.

"No. We run it through the usual procedures." Broyles face started to turn a shade of red Barbara was very familiar with. "But, for all we know, the kid could've mailed it before we arrested him. Maybe I'll ask him. Shake the little bastard up."

Barbara knew the risk of pushing any more, but her mouth started to work before her brain told it not to. "What if nothing falls out?"

He gave her a long look, and she anticipated the explosion that never came. When he spoke, he enunciated each word very slowly. "Then we'll give it some time. Sooner or later it will become very clear whether this is a crank or not."

Leaving the Chief's office, Barbara wondered about the confusion of feelings she'd experienced since this case started. Identifying with the victims. Jumping every time she heard a noise in the night. Doubting a case that was looking pretty rock solid. Maybe her hesitance about Wertco wasn't as impersonal as she'd like to believe. *Is he really innocent? Or is it only my inability to accept the possibility of his guilt?*

Good question, and she had less than seventy-two hours to find the answer. The most logical place to start was with the kid.

She quickly passed through the various channels of authority at the county jail and was told to wait in the cheerless, drab room where inmates met with their attorneys. Listening to the distant sounds of cell doors clanging and leather heels scrapping on concrete, Barbara tried not to think about the grimy, institutional gray walls or the stale, sour smell of fear and sweat. Or how it might feel to sit in this room, innocent of the crime you're charged with and no hope in proving it.

Her hope for Wertco had ridden its own ups and downs as she'd found nothing to clear him, and she wondered if she should just quit. Let it all go. *It's getting to you, Hobkins. It really is. One minute you're desperate to clear him. The next, you're ready to call the hangman.*

The hollow sound of the jailer's key announced Royce Wertco's arrival. When he shuffled into the room, he looked at Barbara with wild, accusing eyes. He hadn't changed much in three years. The same lank, dirty blonde hair in disarray, but he had a little more look of a man about him now—thicker neck, harder jaw. Despite those hints of approaching adulthood, Barbara still saw that young, scared-shitless teenager in his hazel eyes. A rank odor of nervous sweat filling the room confirmed her suspicion that he was not as confident as his swagger.

The guard nodded to Barbara, then stepped back and stood with his back to the door.

"How're you doing, Royce?" She motioned for him to sit in one of the battered metal chairs.

"Great. Just great." His voice rang with sarcasm.

Barbara took a chair opposite him and placed a folder on the scarred wooden table.

"There are no formal charges yet." She kept her voice crisp, choosing to ignore his hostility. "Perhaps if you'd cooperate."

"Don't hand me that shit." Royce stood abruptly, knocking his chair over with a loud clatter.

The guard took a step forward, and Barbara motioned him back with a wave of her hand. Royce seemed oblivious as he continued his rant. "You're just itchin' to pin this on me. You cops've been on my ass about everything since that first time."

Barbara stood and looked directly into his wild eyes. "Peddle your snow job to someone else, Royce. You've made your own trouble and you know it."

Tension hummed in the room, while Royce appeared to consider her words. Then he picked up his chair and dropped into the seat with an air of defiance.

Barbara leaned over the table. "Your smart mouth and hot temper won't do you a damn bit of good. Unless you want us to believe you DID kill Aimee Nelson."

His head jerked up as if he'd been hit with a cattle prod, and his eyes locked with hers. "I didn't do it! Does that make any fuckin' difference?"

"Not a bit." She fought for control, determined not to let him get to her. "Unless you can prove it."

She straightened and crossed her arms across her chest. "Now I suggest you do some serious thinking about whether you want me to walk out of here or not."

Royce looked at his hands, balled into fists in his lap, shot a quick glance at the guard, then raised his eyes to Barbara's. "All right. Let's talk."

"Fine." She sat back down and opened the folder, sliding a paper out. "First thing to consider is an alibi. You sure you didn't talk to anyone Friday afternoon before six-thirty?"

Royce leaned his elbows on the table and propped his head in his hands. "I said it all a hundred times. I just wandered around. Then went to her house. Wanted to talk to her. But I changed my mind. So I went to the park and just sat. After a while I went and got my money from old man Barnett."

"Okay. We'll drop that for now. But think of anybody who was at the park. If you saw them, they might remember you." Barbara shuffled through the papers in the folder and took out a black and white photograph.

"Take a look at this." She pushed it across to him. "Recognize it?"

Royce studied the picture for a moment, then shrugged and handed it back. His expression never changed.

"You mother identified the quilt as one she gave you a few months ago." Barbara continued to watch him. "It was covering Aimee Nelson's body."

A vein throbbed in his neck as he gripped the edge of the table. "I took that quilt to the lake weeks ago. When I left, I forgot the damn thing."

"Who was with you at the lake?"

Royce wiped at the sheen of sweat on his face. "Friends."

"I need names, Royce. Maybe one of them took the quilt."

"Why are you doing this?"

The question and a softness in his eyes touched a section of her heart she thought was securely closed off. "I honestly don't know." She slid the picture back in the folder. "Maybe I just need a little more convincing."

She stood and nodded to the guard, then turned back to the kid. "Send for me if you think of anything that'll help."

She half believed Wertco's story about the quilt. There must be a way of proving that the one covering Aimee Nelson's body wasn't his. At times, it seemed almost ludicrous to be hung up on that one simple aspect of the case. But beyond the macabre feeling of finding something made with endless hours of love and devotion at a brutal murder scene, Barbara felt the quilt's owner could provide the name of the killer.

Barbara had just returned to the office when Keith walked in.

"Where've you been?" he asked.

"What's up?"

Keith shrugged out of his jacket and hung it up. "Just talked to the Chief. The DA wants to go to the Grand Jury."

"When?"

"Soon as he can arrange it." Keith lowered his bulk to his chair. "In the meantime, the Chief wants us to handle a burglary. Just came in this morning."

"What about this case?"

"He's ready to wrap it up. Vaughn and Richards are going to pull in the last few details."

Barbara rocked her chair on its back legs, her head spinning. A new case. The Grand Jury. Could Royce have pulled one over on her again? *No. Damn it. It's more than gullibility and emotionalism. Too many things don't fit. Especially Royce. Why the hell did I spend all those years studying psychology if nobody's going to believe me?*

"You want to take a look at this burglary report?" Keith asked, tossing the folder across to her.

She picked up the folder, but didn't open it. "Could you cover this?"

"What the hell?" For a moment he just stared at her. "That's not like you."

"Please, Keith. I wouldn't ask if it wasn't important. I'll step in if you need me."

He motioned for her to pass the report back. "We could both end up with our ass in a sling, you know."

"Not if we're careful."

Friends of Royce Wertco weren't easy to find. Barbara didn't think they would be considering they were one jump ahead of the law and looking over their shoulders every step of the way. The two she managed to locate that afternoon slammed doors in her face.

Thursday, she didn't find anybody, and Keith started making noises like he wanted to back out of their agreement. She finally talked him into one more day.

Her hopes were fading faster than Clinton's Q rating when she finally located Al Gardner. It was late Friday afternoon, and he was at the gas station where he worked. When he worked.

Barbara approached the burly man in greasy overalls who was bent over the open hood of a car. "I need to talk to you about Royce Wertco." She showed him her ID.

"I don't know nothing about Royce." Gardner barely paused in his work. "Ain't seen him in months."

"Be a little more specific." Barbara stepped into the garage, out of the glare of the sun.

"I told ya, Lady. It's been a long time." He leaned his elbow on the fender, his eyes scanning her from head to toe, then focusing on her chest. "Only folks I keep track of are female."

Barbara pulled her jacket tighter. "You didn't see him last Friday?"

"He's bad news. I been steerin' clear of him." Gardner picked up a wrench and turned back to the engine. "You're wastin' your time."

"Tell me about that time last spring when you went to the lake with Royce."

"What's this?" Gardner looked up at her again. "I'm gonna be in trouble over a little party?"

The hostility was so strong it washed over her in a chill wave. "No trouble. Just trying to clear up a little detail."

"What detail?"

"Did Royce bring a quilt out there?"

"Yeah. Girls were always bitchin' about getting dirty. Royce said his old lady had lots of blankets. He'd bring one."

"Remember what it looked like?"

Gardner shrugged. "I dunno. It was just an old blanket. Nothing special."

Barbara took the picture of the quilt from her pocket and showed it to him. "Could this be it?"

"Might have... No. It was just a plain old blanket."

"You sure?" Desperation made her voice rise.

"Hey, Lady. I'm doin' my best. How do you 'spect me to remember somthin' from so long ago." Gardner walked over to the workbench and rummaged in a dented metal toolbox, pulling out a rusty wrench.

"Thanks for you help," Barbara said. "Call if you think of anything else." She left her card on the faded pad protecting the car's glossy green fender.

"Sure." The man didn't even bother to turn around.

Easing her car into traffic, Barbara realized how ridiculous it was to put Garner in the role of the concerned citizen cooperating with the police. Not even to help a one-time friend.

Maybe Keith was right. She should forget it. Accept the inevitable. The case against Wertco was getting stronger and stronger, while she was spinning her wheels.

No. I will not give up. She drummed her fingertips on the steering wheel as she waited for the light to change. *You just need a little time away from it all. Get your head thinking clearly again.*

She considered her options and decided that a nice hot bath and the latest offering from her favorite romance author would do.

Smiling, she pulled into her parking space and headed toward her apartment. It would be good to be a normal human being for a change. She unlocked the outer door and stepped in to be greeted by the pungent aroma of curry. Dinner was on at the Delphi's.

Halfway up the stairway, she heard the front door open again, and she turned to see who'd come in. No one was there. The sudden silence was unnerving, but then she realized it was probably Franklin leaving. He had the other ground floor apartment and constantly bitched about the smell. In her estimation it beat the hell out of the stale smoke that permeated his place.

Stepping out on the second floor landing, Barbara heard a faint rustle of sound from down the stairway. HAD someone come in? As fear traced a cold finger up her spine, she whirled. Emptiness greeted her.

Then she heard another sound. Louder. This time from in front. When she turned back and saw Mr. Gilroy locking his apartment door, she swallowed her anxiety. He looked up and smiled, the action making him look like an elderly pixie. "Good evening, Miss Hobkins."

"Hello." Her relief came out in one big sigh. Dear, sweet Mr. Gilroy with his very proper manner was as harmless as a Teddy Bear. "Going out for the evening?"

"Yes. And you should, too. No way for a pretty little thing like you to live. Working all the time. Ought to have some nice young man to take care of you. Give you a baby or two."

It was his standard line every time they met in the hall, but somehow it never seemed to grate coming from him. Maybe because, unlike her mother, he didn't have a personal stake in the outcome. Barbara smiled and unlocked her door. "I'll see about that, Mr. Gilroy. First chance I get."

He doffed his black derby, then moved down the hall.

After stepping inside the apartment, she locked the door and threw the dead-bolt.

He waited until he was sure the old man had gone, then stepped from the shadows and went back inside. In the hallway outside her door, he paused and listened. Nothing. Quietly, he took the knob in his sweaty palm and turned. Locked. Should he try to force it? *You jerk. She'll hear. Have time to get ready.*

Frustrated, he stood with his fists clenched at his side. Why'd that old fart have to show up like that? He'd almost had her. Came so close... He pounded one tight fist against his thigh. He felt trapped by forces within as well as out. His brain boiled, seethed, threatened to overflow.

He knew he had to get away before darkness enfolded him completely. He'd just have to wait until opportunity presented itself again.

Chapter Fifteen

Saturday, October 30—Twin Lakes

Gene had plenty of time before picking up Barbara. *Plenty of time and nothing to do.* Maybe he should take the opportunity to go to Tom's. If it was too difficult to be there, he could always use his date as an excuse to leave.

Tom had called the other day. Wondered why he hadn't come over since... Gene couldn't think about that terrible day, or the reasons why the thought of going to Tom's filled him with such dread. Better to keep them packed away with all the other ugly things in his life, like Nancy.

Gene eased the car into the driveway and glanced at the house. It looked lonely and deserted in the gathering darkness. *You can do this. It's just comforting a friend.* Then he got out of the car, squared his shoulders, and walked in.

An eerie feeling of déjà vu washed over him, and he had to fight the ghosts of that terrible day. He forced himself to see the den as it was now. *Just a room.*

It worked. The anxiety subsided, and he called out, "Anybody home?"

"Gene?" Tom emerged from the hallway. "I was just back there... looking through some things." He nodded toward the bedroom.

"Want to finish?"

"I'll have a drink instead." Tom walked over to the portable bar by the fireplace. "Join me?"

"Sure."

Tom brought drinks over, then lowered himself into the overstuffed chair with a sigh. "What brings you by?"

Gene sat on the end of the sofa and swirled the amber liquid in his glass. "Wanted to see how you're doing."

Tom shrugged.

"Maybe you should come back to work."

"I'm not ready."

"How long?" Gene looked quickly at his friend, then away.

"As long as I need."

"Don't take forever. Nobody's worth that."

"What?" Tom looked at him as if he'd been slapped. "How can you be so callous?"

"I'm sorry if it sounded that way." Gene sighed. "Just trying to be realistic. Shit happens and we have to get past it."

"Oh, I see." Tom slapped his drink down on the table so hard liquid sloshed over the edge. "You're the expert on how everyone should live their lives."

"That's not what I meant."

"Then clarify it for me." Tom rose and waved a trembling hand at the other man. "What profound tidbit of wisdom do you have for me?"

Gene set his drink down. *Would the better part of discretion be to just walk out? Leave it alone?* He looked at Tom, who shifted his weight from one foot to another in quick, jerky moves.

Okay. The SOB wants the truth. I'll give him the truth. "The only way I could get over Nancy-"

"Oh, Christ." Tom whirled and stomped to the other side of the room, then turned and faced him. "Does everything have to be about that?"

"It's not about *that*." Gene stood and took one step toward his friend. "It's about reality. Nobody's perfect, Tom. Not Nancy. And not even Susan."

The last few words were spoken softly, but they echoed through the house, coming back to assault Tom over and over again. He covered his ears. Then he whirled, his face contorted with rage. "Get out. You don't know a thing about Susan."

Tom picked up a small glass jar and hurled it.

Only Gene's quick reflexes kept him from catching the missile full on the face. "I'm sorry, Tom. I didn't mean-"

"Leave me alone!"

Gene backed away. God, he hadn't meant for this to happen. He considered making one more appeal, but Tom turned away from him.

With the worst case of shakes he'd had in years, Gene left the house. He got into his car and dropped the keys on the floorboard. Bending over to retrieve them, he banged his head on the dash. "Son of a bitch!" He inserted the key in the ignition with trembling fingers and brought the car to life. Then he leaned against the headrest and tried to figure out how a goodwill mission had turned so ugly.

Maybe he should've waited another couple of weeks. Should've realized Tom's grief was like a huge open sore that didn't need anyone probing at it. But he was only trying to help. And it's not like he'd ever tell Tom about Susan flirting with him. Would never talk about that. But, damn, he didn't want his friend to throw his life away grieving somebody who wasn't exactly faultless.

He put the car in gear and drove to the Lone Star Grill. *Had to take time to settle down before seeing Barbara.*

Leaning close to the mirror, Barbara made one more smooth stroke with the eyeliner. *Perfect.* The fine brown line above her long lashes gave her eyes the depth and intensity of emeralds. She added a final touch of blush across her delicate cheeks and lightly pressed her glistening red lips to a tissue.

It felt good to be away from reports, growling partners, and worries about Royce Wertco. Worrying wasn't accomplishing anything.

The expression on Gene's face when she opened the door to his knock convinced her the extra time with make-up had been worth it. So was the new dress, which, according to the sales clerk who'd talked her into buying it, 'Could drive a man wild.'

Apparently the woman was right about the little black sheath that clung to parts of Barbara even she'd forgotten she had. She smiled at the flush that crept up Gene's face when his eyes moved from the daring neckline to her face.

"Let me get my coat," she said.

"Sure."

"Where are we going?" She let him assist her with the soft, brown suede wrap.

"Do you mind being surprised?"

"Not at all."

He kept up the mystery as they drove out of Twin Lakes, heading toward the distant lights of Dallas. Barbara was pleased. Nothing about the stuffiness of the country club or the blaring noise of the Rooster's Roost appealed to her.

"How's the case going?" Gene asked.

"Depends on your viewpoint."

"It's hard to believe Royce..." Gene let his voice trail off.

"That makes a grand total of two." Barbara laughed. "But I don't want to talk about it. I promised myself a weekend free of frustration."

The pickup that entered the expressway just behind them was easily discounted, considering the number of people who went to Dallas on a Saturday night. The man in the truck silently cursed as he allowed a semi to drift past. It hadn't done any good to follow them. *Should've known better. Shouldn't have waited so long outside the apartment.* If he'd gone in first, he could've left a nice surprise for that big-shot principal. *I know what he thinks of me. Nothin' but a piece of shit to be wiped off those fancy shoes of his.*

Once Barbara and Gene passed through the entry of Bugatti's On The River, she felt another layer of frustration lift. A subdued hum of conversation flowed pleasantly from the dining area, and the enticing aroma of garlic and olive oil wafted from the kitchen.

A Maitre 'D in black pants, a starched white shirt, and a bold red bowtie escorted them to a table in an alcove. The seating afforded some privacy, and Barbara settled into the chair with a deep sigh.

Wine was ordered. Then appetizers. Then more wine. She wondered if she'd make it through dinner without passing out. But it was hard not to get caught up in the magic of candlelight, crystal, and the haunting music brought to life by the nimble fingers of a bearded man who moved from table to table with his Mandolin.

The waiter set warm plates of Veal Marsala in front of them, then made a discreet exit. Barbara watched Gene take a bite, wondering about the quiet that seemed to wash over him in waves. She'd noticed it in the car first, like he'd drifted away for a few minutes. Then it happened here too. *What thoughts could be knitting his brows together in such a frown?*

Instinctively, she reached out to touch his hand. "What's wrong?"

"Nothing." He shrugged and glanced away. "I mean, hell, things just still cave in on me."

"I'm sorry. I keep forgetting. Part of the armor I wear." She squeezed his hand. "How's Tom?"

"Probably okay until a few hours ago. I tried to help."

"What happened?"

"I leaned on him a little too hard."

"What about?"

Gene's response was lost as the minstrel came to their table and bowed deeply to Barbara, never missing a beat in his tune. The song was very suggestive, even without words, and she felt Gene's pulse quicken under her fingertips. She smiled. *Maybe if they really tried, they could put both their personal demons to rest and let something else happen tonight.*

Turmoil clouded Gene's eyes again as the musician wandered to another table, the strains of a melody trailing behind along with the faint scent of his cologne.

Barbara tugged on Gene's hand. "Would you rather leave?"

"No. I'll like myself better if we stay."

His spirits seemed to lift while they finished their dinners. Later, they moved to the lounge area where a small band played. Gene held out a hand to her, "Shall we?"

They stepped onto the dance floor, and she slipped into his arms. He held her gently at first, savoring her softness and the faint, yet tantalizing aroma of musk that drifted up to him. As the music faded, he pulled her tight. For a moment, he almost forgot they weren't alone.

Then he relaxed his hold and took a step back. There was a faint dreaminess in the eyes that met his and returned an unmistakable message.

"Ready to go?" he asked.

She nodded.

In the car, Barbara settled back against the seat, thankful for the cool evening breeze that cleared her head. They drove in a companionable silence and, sitting close to Gene's warmth, she let her mind drift.

She never felt this way with Roger. Silences between them were always strained, and she struggled to fill them before he accused her of being preoccupied with her job. *Why was it such an important factor to him? It didn't seem to bother Gene. Or was that only because it hadn't interfered yet?*

Startled by the thought, she looked at his strong profile. He turned and gave her a smile. "You okay?" he asked.

"I am now." She nestled her head against the back of the seat.

As if some secret signal gave mutual consent, Gene braked the car in front of his house. Inside, he went to the kitchen to make coffee, while Barbara sat on the couch, kicking off her shoes and tucking her feet under her.

Gene came back in, bearing two large mugs. "Hope you don't mind instant. It's all I ever use. Senseless to brew coffee for one person."

She took the mug. "One of the many problems of single life."

A shadow crossed his face, and he glanced away. Just when she thought she was getting a handle on him, this happened again. "Is there a problem?" she asked, gently.

"No." He emphasized the word with a little laugh, but it sounded a bit strained.

"Is this business with Tom still bothering you?"

"Some." He took a swallow of coffee. "I think I was a bit of an ass."

"I'm sure it wasn't that bad."

He sighed. "Yeah. I think it was."

He started his narrative in faltering words, and she settled back to listen. As he talked, his voice rose and fell like waves washing up on a beach.

The words brought the whole scene alive in her mind and gave her a bitter taste of his self-recrimination. She'd felt the same way almost ten years ago when Marcy's mother died. The woman had suffered for a long time in a futile battle against breast cancer, and Barbara had tried to console her friend with the platitude, 'At least she isn't suffering any more.'

Despite being well intentioned, the comment had touched off a volcanic eruption of anger in Marcy, leaving Barbara feeling twisted and helpless inside. A few days later, Marcy apologized for the flare up, and Barbara was relieved to be on even footing with her friend again. But the incident had taught her how bumbling one human being can be without even realizing it.

"There you have it," Gene finished. "The ruination of a friendship."

"I'm sure he'll realize you meant well once he has a chance to think about it."

"Maybe."

He reached out and twisted one copper curl around his finger. She felt a rush of anticipation when his eyes softened and he leaned forward. He ran his fingers across the top of her nearly bare shoulder.

A delicious tingling followed the trail of his hand, and Barbara's breath caught in her throat. *He's going to kiss me.*

As if reading her mind, he lowered his lips to hers. They were warm, soft, and the kiss teased. She felt an urgency for more and leaned into him. He cupped the back of her head, and the contact was no longer tentative. His lips crushed hers, while his tongue found entry. His fingers trailed across the bare skin on her neck, slowly finding their way to the edge of her low-cut dress. Heat surged as her nipples peaked against the softness of the fabric. *Oh, God, touch me before I explode.*

As if hearing her silent message, Gene cupped one breast in his large hand and ran his thumb over the hardness. Barbara sighed behind the kiss, and he removed his hand to lean over and press his body against hers. Any possibility of ending it there faded with a new rise of passion. He pulled away slightly and looked at her, chest heaving. "Should we finish this in the bedroom?"

"Absolutely."

Chapter Sixteen

Sunday, October 31—Twin Lakes

He smiled as he put the newspaper on the bed, keeping the bold headlines visible: SUSPECT ARRAIGNED IN BRUTAL TWIN LAKES MURDERS. *Sometimes people can be so stupid.* He'd tried to tell her. *Didn't she get it?*

At first, it bothered him when they arrested that kid. How could he take credit for what he didn't do? But now? *What the fuck?* There was no heat out there now. He could go back to his old place.

There was plenty of time now. No reason to rush. He could enjoy it. Play with it. Savor it.

Filled with a sense of well being, he carefully prepared for the evening. He'd missed his place. That was one of the things he hated most about that cop. She'd kept him from going. But not now. Now he was free as a bird.

Anticipation stirred his breath as he packed a black suit and white shirt neatly at the bottom of the gym bag. It had been a long time. For the past three nights, he'd been unable to sleep, prowling the house in a state of suppressed sexual excitement.

But tonight was his.

Barbara watched Brenda put the finishing touches on the costume for Keith, Jr. He was ten and had earlier stated that this was his last year to go out Trick or Treating. He was growing up now. Too old for baby stuff. Although it was fun to dress up like his favorite sport celebrity. This year it was Emmit Smith.

Watching him trundle out, football in one hand, orange bag in the other, Barbara wondered what it would be like to have a child. If she'd 'done the right thing,' as her mother so aptly put it ten years ago, she could be taking her own kid out tonight.

"He's something, isn't he?" Keith said as the door closed behind his wife and son.

"You're lucky."

"Not sure luck has anything to do with it."

"You got Brenda."

"There is that."

Loud voices called 'Trick or Treat' from outside. Keith grabbed a handful of candy from the nearby dish and opened the door. Barbara snagged a miniature

Hershey bar and ate it, while Keith dispensed the candy and good cheer. After the kids left, he turned to her. "Something going on with you?"

"I don't know." She rolled the wrapper into a small ball. "Just wondering when my luck's going to change."

"What about Roger?"

"History."

"Oh. Didn't realize." He glanced at his shoes, then back to her. "Sorry."

"I've had a couple of dates with Gene Wilkins."

"Oh. Wondered when I saw him at your place that night."

Keith looked so patently uncomfortable that Barbara had to laugh. "We can skip my love life if you like."

She didn't miss the obvious relief in his expression before he turned to respond to the latest wave of kids. Maybe it was too soon to talk about Gene, anyway. Last night had been good. In some ways, even more exciting than the first good year with Roger. But even in the midst of that most intimate of activities, she'd felt a reserve in Gene.

Is it because our relationship's still so new? Or because of the tragedy that first brought them together? Or is there another reason I'm not even seeing? Maybe some old baggage associated with his divorce?

Barbara shook her head and joined Keith at the door. She'd come here to share in the fun of the holiday, a good antidote to the frustrations of the job and her life. She wasn't going to scuttle the opportunity with endless mind games.

Rosie tucked a black curl behind her ear and watched the man as he made his third pass down the street. He seemed to be making a careful selection of the merchandise, like a vulture circling a dead cat on the road.

For an instant, Rosie's radar was alerted. A funny hunch that... *Oh, what the hell. If he picks me, I could very well end up with an all-nighter. He wouldn't be shopping so carefully for a quickie. They seldom do.*

She knew he wasn't a cop. She had good radar for that, too. Cops always tried too hard not to look like cops. The act never fooled her. Something always clued her in before she made her approach.

That's what had kept her out of jail for the last three years. Unlike most girls who end up on the streets out of desperation, Rosie came to them for the pure simple fact that she liked it. With an almost ghoulish fascination, she actually enjoyed the games played between John and Girl. She wasn't the victim. He was. A whimpering, slobbering, moronic puppet at her command.

Yes, she enjoyed her work.

This was the end of the week and, like any other working girl, Rosie looked forward to an easy finish. Her face wore a look of smug satisfaction when the John passed up three other girls and stopped in front of her. With hungry appraisal, his pale eyes swept the swell of her ample breasts where the lace of her red chemise ended. Thin lips parted around stained teeth.

For the second time in minutes, Rosie's radar was triggered: an electrifying synoptic leap to the brain with unswerving speed. She should just walk away.

But challenge replaced panic. She would enjoy taking this one down.

Rosie Shiner didn't enjoy much after that. She died at 1:22am.

Chapter Seventeen

Monday, November 1—Twin Lakes

Gene stopped his progress down the hall when he saw Tom heading toward his classroom. It was early yet, and only a few of the most dedicated students were here for special study groups. He let a gang of them pass, then walked to the door his friend had left open. He rapped once on the glass panel and took a single step inside. "Can we talk?"

Tom glanced at him, shrugged, then turned his attention back to the papers he was arranging on his desk.

The silence was unnerving, but at least he didn't say 'no.' Gene took another step forward. "Glad to see you back."

The rustle of papers was the only sound. *Damn!* "Listen, Tom." Gene took a deep breath. "I'm really sorry about the other night."

He waited while Tom stilled his hands before looking at him. It felt like a week before the other man spoke.

"I'm back, Gene. And maybe I did need a push. I don't know. But I'm not sure I can ever get past what you said."

"I didn't-"

"Stop." Tom held up one hand, the overhead light glinting off the metal watch-band. "No discussion. I know you've been jaded since Nancy left. So I'll chalk it up to that. But don't you ever say anything about Susan again. You didn't *know* her."

"Tom, I-"

"No more. Subject closed." Tom sat down at his desk and opened a textbook.

Gene waited a moment, hoping his friend would reconsider, but Tom didn't raise his eyes.

Barbara caught Broyles on his way out of his office. He looked like a bear in his heavy overcoat and held an abused briefcase in one hand as a barrier to anyone who dared to deter him from an appointment.

"Got a minute?" she asked.

"Barely." He glanced at his watch, then back at her. "What do you need?"

"I'm still not convinced Wertco's our man."

"Despite the witness putting him at the girl's house shortly before the murder? And his prints at the scene?" The Chief's glare was murderous. "And let's not forget motive. 'Rejected lover gets revenge' to quote our local Washington Post wannabe."

"Am I being paid to think? Or do you just want a drone to follow orders?"

The moment hung in suspended animation as Broyles loomed over her, a tic in his cheek testifying to the effort of his control. Then he pushed Barbara into his office and slammed the door. "You got two minutes."

"There are too many loose ends. The quilt-"

"Probably unrelated."

"The panty business at the school."

Broyles sighed. "Wertco could've-"

"But it's outside his normal mode of behavior."

"This where the psychology lecture begins? What the hell do you know about his 'mode of behavior?'"

Barbara clenched her fists and held her arms rigid. "You can't deny this case has had a strong psychological undercurrent from the beginning. A normal, rational human being did not kill those victims. And it wasn't a seventeen-year-old kid either."

"Come off it, Hobkins. Isn't it time you quit mothering him?"

His words cut her to the bone, and she fought to keep her voice at a rational level. "I'm not arguing because it's Royce Wertco. I'd think this no matter who we had behind bars. The killer is still out there. And I don't think he's finished yet."

"God!" Broyles slammed his briefcase down and slumped in the chair behind his desk. "Maybe the commissioner's right about women on the job."

Barbara abruptly turned away and stalked to the window. She would not respond. Would not validate his attitude that way.

"Okay, Hobkins." His voice was calmer now. "If the kid didn't do it, who did?"

She turned to face him again. "Could be Earl Avery."

"Who the hell is he?"

"The gravedigger."

"Not again. I told you before, you can't suspect someone just because you don't like the color of his eyes."

Barbara stormed to the desk. "I'm better than that, and you know it."

The Chief stood slowly and leveled a fierce gaze on her. "Watch your mouth."

She clenched her jaw and returned his gaze, "I apologize for my rudeness."

"If you think you're right, prove it. Otherwise, case closed."

Stiff-lipped, Barbara nodded and walked out of the office on trembling legs.

Of all the arrogant, insufferable... How dare he? To even insinuate that my femininity's interfering in the case. She thought she'd put that problem to rest a long time ago. But apparently, it still lurked, ready to crop up to suit the convenience of whoever needed it at the moment.

Fine. If he wants to dismiss my ideas on that basis, let him. Let him go off to his precious meeting and reassure the commissioner that the residents of Twin Lakes have nothing more to worry about. I don't care.

But the problem was, she did care. Not about proving that she was right and he was wrong. That was incidental. But she had a responsibility for the safety of the people. She felt the weight of that responsibility fall heavily on her shoulders every time she passed a young woman on the street.

Not able to resign herself to the confines of her office, Barbara left the station and walked to the taco stand on the corner. The afternoon sun hung high in a cobalt sky, bathing her in a pleasant warmth that soothed the deep ache of her soul.

For a moment, she wished she could chuck it all and go back to a time when life seemed much simpler. When she believed she'd marry Roger and have his children. When she seemed happy with that prospect. It would be nice to go to his place today and forget her troubles in a long, leisurely ride on that gentle sorrel mare.

Ordering a soft drink, Barbara took a deep breath and leaned her elbows on the counter. There was a unique vividness and clarity of color to the world on bright days like today, and she marveled at people who thought there was no autumn in Texas. There was: you just had to look for it in different ways.

The thoughts of Roger surprised her. Especially after the other night with Gene. She thought it would be a simple matter to dismiss Roger from her mind, after dismissing him from her life. But memories crowded her heart. Good times they'd shared before it went bad.

And this personal confusion wasn't helping with the job. How on earth could she focus on proving the kid's innocence with her mind straying like a maverick steer?

Barbara glanced across the street and felt a sudden inner chill when her gaze touched on a vaguely familiar figure. The man turned quickly before she could see his face. Then a cloud passed over the sun, casting a surrealistic cover of gray over the street.

She no longer felt warm and welcome outside. Shuddering involuntarily, Barbara turned and hurried back to the station, seeking the security of a bright bustling interior. Opening the door, she tried to shake the feeling of wary apprehension that followed her. *What's gotten into you, girl? You haven't done this since trading ghost stories at camp.*

When she walked into the office, she found Keith buried under an array of reports and the remains of lunch scattered across his desk.

"Anything new?" She sat at her desk and idly toyed with a pile of yellow pencil stubs, the last remnants of unease making her fidget.

"Hmmm, just a sec." A moment later, he handed a paper across to her. "Crosby just brought this in. Might be the first step in tying the Wertco kid to the Delgrave murder. Seems like he skipped school that day. And he doesn't have anyone to verify his whereabouts."

Barbara's heart sank as she scanned the report. Maybe her instincts *were* wrong, and she should do with them what Keith and the Chief so often suggested. Wertco did have the opportunity. A neighbor just back from a business trip said he'd seen someone who looked like the kid in the area the morning Susan was killed. But he'd left that same morning. He didn't even know about the murder until the officer came to his door yesterday. But, what could Wertco's motive be? Beyond the obvious connection of teacher and student, there was no indication he even knew the Delgraves.

She looked at Keith. "What do you think?"

"I don't know. It's nothing we can take to court." He leaned back and cradled the back of his head in his hands. "Sometimes I wonder if we're all too eager to hook the first ass, any ass, just to get it over with. Then again, we can't ignore evidence, even circumstantial."

"But it's not adding up. Wertco isn't the type to kill that way."

"We can't 'type' the guy who's responsible. There's nothing normal about the homicides from the get-go. If we categorize things ABC, the killer's gonna throw us a Z."

"So we just quit?" Barbara threw up her arms in exasperation. "Not me. I'm not off the case until the jury tells me so."

Keith shrugged. "Suit yourself. Me, I'm going home and spend some time with my wife and kids. That is, if they still remember who I am."

Barbara sat at her desk a long time after her partner left. Just the simple act of trying to think drove her nuts. She did all this thinking, and speculating, and wondering, and what good did it do? All she came up with was a bunch of theories. Time was running out for her and for Royce Wertco.

Remembering what the Chief said about proof, Barbara decided it was time to take some action. Maybe going to Avery's crib would shake him up.

Having a definite plan, Barbara felt the doubts recede as she locked sensitive files in her bottom drawer and grabbed her jacket. At the door of her office, she hesitated. Maybe she should run this past the Chief. Follow procedure.

To hell with procedure.

"Jee-sus," Barbara said. She eased the Datsun into what passed as a driveway and stared at the yard. The entire lot was buried in a mountain of junk: rusted bedsprings, old buckets, a couple of dented car fenders, and an ancient eight-cylinder engine mounted on cinderblocks. Those were just the big pieces.

Her two brief encounters with Earl Avery hadn't prepared her for anything like this. True, she didn't expect a mansion, but this was incredible.

A large two-story house, once grand and regal, now stood like the victim of some cruel and vicious assault. Paint peeled from every surface, eaves sagged, and it was encased, or possibly held upright, by the tomb of junk.

She braked the car and stared. *Keith will never believe this.*

The woman who answered Barbara's knock appeared to be an extension of the same gross neglect suffered by the house. Unwashed hair hung in strings, touching the tops of shoulders rounded by the weight of a heavy, moth-eaten black shawl.

"Does Earl Avery live here?" Barbara felt the decrepit porch shift under her feet, the creak of old wood making her wonder if it would give.

"Sometimes." The woman's face was a mirror of disgust. "Whatta you want with him?"

Barbara flashed her shield. "Just a few questions. He here now?"

The woman shook her head. "You can ask me."

Cold blue eyes, just like Earl's, bored through Barbara. She shifted on the rickety porch. "I'd rather talk to him."

"I told you. He ain't here." The woman took a step closer. "He was. But he took off a bit ago."

"Do you know when he'll be back?" Barbara tried not to look beyond the woman's large frame to the cancerous interior of the house. A sour odor wafted out the open door.

"You still botherin' 'bout that kid what got herself kilt? We already told you he was home that night." Layers of saliva built up in the cracked corners of the woman's mouth. "What would Earl know about her anyway? He just works around the school. Don't mean he knows nothin' 'bout them kids, does it?"

"Not at all." Barbara softened her voice, hoping to calm the tension building in the old woman. "This is just routine."

"I dunno when he'll be back."

Barbara made an effort not to stare at Mrs. Avery as a long-ago memory came to mind. One year, her Sunday school class had visited a nursing home to sing Christmas carols. It was Barbara's first visit to a place like that, and she'd recoiled from the people strapped to chairs, heads lolling. Despite the revulsion, her eyes had been drawn to a woman's crust-covered scalp, visible through thin orange hair. When she asked what happened to the old lady, she was told the woman was just old and sick. Many years later, she'd learned the real reason for such a condition. It wasn't age and sickness: it was filth and neglect.

The sour smell of Mrs. Avery's breath in her face brought Barbara back to the present. "If he should come-"

The loud screech of tires on asphalt cut Barbara off. She turned to see Avery's truck rumble to the curb.

Earl recognized the woman on his porch even before the truck came to a full stop, and a shiver passed through his body. *What the hell is she doing here?*

A smile pasted on his face, he made his way up the front walk. "Well, well, well. Look who's come'a callin'. The police lady."

"Earl, you tell this woman she ain't got no right botherin' us," Mrs. Avery said quickly.

A strange look passed from mother to son before Earl responded, and Barbara felt a prickle of discomfort when his gaze came to rest on her. "That's okay," he said. "We gotta be nice to police officers."

"I need to go over your story again. About the afternoon Aimee Nelson was killed-"

"We already done that." Earl licked his lips. "Didn't you check it out?"

"I just need to hear it again, in case there's a detail we missed."

"Let's see." His eyes held hers with a mocking expression. "Like I said, I picked up those trees at three-thirty. Fall's the best time to plant trees, ya know."

Barbara turned a page in her notebook.

"I signed for them trees. Did you check that out?" The indulgent smile playing around his mouth didn't change, and he didn't wait for her to answer. "Then I worked over at the school 'til after five-thirty."

"You stayed there the whole time?" Barbara purposely allowed a hint of threat into her voice. "Or did you get someone else to do your work?"

"Ask the principal. He saw me."

"I did, Mr. Avery. But he saw you at five-thirty. Aimee was killed at six." A gust of wind blew across the porch, lifting, then dropping the notebook pages. Barbara pushed a strand of hair off her face. "What did you do after you finished the trees?"

"I didn't do nothin' but come home." His eyes flashed quickly to his mother. "Watched TV then went to bed. Just like she said."

"Thank you for cooperating again." Barbara closed her book and took one step off the porch. Then she paused. "You will be available for further questions?"

The only response was a slight tensing around the cold eyes regarding her, then Earl turned and entered the house. His mother barely made it in before the door slammed with a resounding boom.

Back in her car, Barbara stared at the house with a mixed feeling of excitement and dread. There was something about this guy, something more than her suspicions. And certainly more than any evidence she'd scrapped up against him.

But a small part of her wished she were wrong. At this point, Barbara wasn't sure she was a match for the sickness simmering just below the surface of this man.

Chapter Eighteen

Monday, November 1—Dallas

Yance Cleary, short, balding, and going to fat, had always wanted to dabble in real estate. He enjoyed dazzling his friends with talk of impressive investments and margins of earnings. He figured it would make up for his other deficits of character. But the fact was, he didn't have many friends. They were limited to anyone he could get to listen to whatever line of bullshit he was slinging at the moment. That's the way he'd survived in school. Fast-talking his way out of trouble with the teachers and into some kind of acceptance with the other kids.

Some things never change.

In his own mind, he had the real-estate game all figured out. It was a simple matter of picking up a single piece of property, sell it for a profit, then do the same thing over again. He'd left the hills of West Virginia with this in mind, tired of working the production line at Owens and having heard there were fortunes just waiting to be made in Dallas.

But his fortune was still a long way off.

His first investment had bombed. It was an old two-story Victorian house that hosted a variety of unsuccessful business ventures. Cleary, for once, found himself easy prey for someone else's scam.

The guy who operated the now defunct florist business had convinced him he was selling the house for expansion reasons. 'Business just outgrew the location' and all that shit. With a paved drive in front and plenty of rear-access parking, Cleary thought he was getting a steal. That was two years ago. The property proved to be a genuine tar baby that stuck to his ass, and he spent a great deal of time looking to unload it on just the right sucker.

Living entailed money, and the house was too damn big to keep running, so Cleary kept himself in food and a one-bedroom apartment by tending bar in a sleazy dump on Greenville Avenue. It was a good place to meet suckers. It was providential that a Mr. Donald C. Simpson had wandered into the Pink Lady last night. Cleary recognized the symptoms right away: the too new clothes, the expansive manner that fell a trifle short. Above all, the over-anxious look in Simpson's eyes as he talked of being a land developer from Des Moines.

Cleary wiped his hands on his once-white apron. *Land developer, my ass. Bet the only time he ever saw Des Moines was from the tail end of a corn wagon.*

"Well, Mr. Simpson. Seems like we're in the same business." Cleary moved down the bar and brought out a bottle of Kentucky bourbon. "Yance Cleary's my name and this here's my place. I got a little proposition you might be interested in."

He devoted the next hour to pouring bourbon down Simpson and singing the praises of the old house. He conveniently omitted the ratty interior, the crappy location, and the exorbitant utility bills.

It was an hour well spent. Before the bottle was empty, Cleary had his prize sucker hooked, netted, and nearly bagged. The man was so impressed that he wanted to see the property first thing in the morning. Clearly made a vague reference to another deal that was still pending. He could show the house in the afternoon.

Cleary dragged his ass out of bed by nine and was ready to head out by ten. It'd been months since he'd been to the house. He figured the least he could do was sweep out the rat shit before Simpson came. If all went as planned and this dumb bastard had any money, Cleary would be on his way to Houston this time next week. Out of the real estate business for good and into a real moneymaker. Oil.

It was unseasonably cold and the sky threatened rain, so Cleary pulled on a filthy overcoat before quietly closing his apartment door. He was two months behind on the rent and careful to avoid the landlady. He hated bedding the skuzzy old whore, but it was better than being tossed out.

He eased the dirty brown Buick against the curb and got out, closing the door gently. If he slammed it too hard, the cracked window would fall inside the door panel. First thing he was going to do if he closed this deal was to get rid of this heap.

At the house, Cleary pulled into the rear parking area, killed the engine, and got out. He hurried to the back door, holding his coat tight against the wind. He touched the padlock, and it fell open in his hand. "Shit. Damn kid's've been here again."

The first time he'd found the place broken into, it was littered with empty bottles, a few odd articles of clothing, and lots of used rubbers. It also reeked with the wet-rope smell of pot

The next time he found it open, the place was clean. In fact, he'd wondered if it wasn't cleaner than the way he left it.

Cleary wasn't really worried about the intruders, other than the usual nuisance factor. There wasn't anything to steal, unless they pried the molding from the doorjambs. Even the upstairs rooms were bare, so Cleary hadn't seen any reason to report the break-ins. It wouldn't do any good anyway. Cops wouldn't do anything, except offer the astute observation that kids today don't have any respect.

Hell, he didn't have to hear it from a cop to recognize the truth.

He pushed the door open, expecting the worst, and was surprised to find the place clean again. Not even a used tissue on the floor. *Must've misjudged my mysterious guests the first time. Maybe I should leave them a twenty toward their next party. Who knows? Might even be able to talk them into coming regular. Couldn't hire a cleaning lady for that amount.*

He climbed the rickety stairs that creaked under his weight. Halfway up, he had to pause to catch his breath. Maybe the upstairs would be clean, too. Then he wouldn't have to do anything before Simpson arrived except dream of Houston, money, and good times.

A strong, rancid odor assaulted his nose as he opened the first door on the landing. It was more than just the mustiness of a room long unused and stronger than the smell of stale urine coming from the bathroom. Breathing through his mouth, Cleary groped the wall for the light switch. Still, the thick, sour smell made his stomach turn, and he automatically drew back as the single bulb dangling from the ceiling came to life. He pressed a wrinkled handkerchief to his nose and stepped inside.

What was once a bare room now contained a small table in one corner piled high with an assortment of blankets. Cleary walked toward the table and absently scuffed the toe of his shoe at a large rusty stain in the middle of the floor. He didn't think the stain had been there before. It looked like a paint spill. *A bitch to clean up.* What caught his eye on the table, turned out to be pieces of nylon cord. Next to the table sat a small, spindly chair, holding a single cotton work glove and more of the shredded yellow cord.

The smell was stronger now, seeping through the handkerchief. Cleary dropped the rope and walked toward the bathroom. "Damn it all to hell," he said. "Probably got a dead varmint in here somewhere."

His senses assaulted by the stench, he swallowed the rising nausea. It smelled worse than any gas station pisser he'd ever been in. He opened the door to a small closet that harbored the rusted water heater. That's where he'd found the dead mice last time. *But shit! They didn't smell half this bad.* He knelt down on his left knee, wincing under its cracking protest, and peered inside.

A frightened, lice-infected rat chose to make his escape as Cleary leaned into the closet. The rat scampered across his outstretched hand. The handkerchief muffled his scream when he sprawled backward on the sticky floor. Then he noticed more of the strange rust-colored stains on the bathroom tile. They formed a trail and disappeared under the door that led to the back room.

What was going on here besides pot parties and orgies?

Sudden fear made Cleary want to race out of there, but morbid curiosity forced him to his feet. He grasped the doorknob and twisted. When he stepped into the room, his eyes widened and he dropped the handkerchief, taking an instinctive step back.

The rotting, nude body of a woman sprawled across the mattress on the floor.

Chapter Nineteen

Tuesday, November 2—Dallas

The large room housing the Crime Against Persons department of Dallas Central buzzed with activity. Desks ringed the room, with four in the middle. Officers talked on phones, shouted back and forth, or criss-crossed the room, their attention buried in their cases.

Detective Harmon rubbed an unsteady hand across his forehead to ease the first throbs of a headache and tried to concentrate on the missing person reports. Reaching the last one, he sighed with a mixture of weakness and exasperation. *This one'll probably remain a Jane Doe. Just like the last one.*

He took a swallow of coffee, now cold, and mentally counted the days until his first chance at retirement. Wouldn't get much. But, hell, maybe it would be worth it. Better to get out with enough for a trailer on the Brazos River than drop dead from the effort of trying to catch these scumbags.

As a rookie, he was told that eventually it would get better, easier to deal with. But the 'it' of death, destruction, suffering, and misery only seemed to feed upon itself and grow, building up layer after crusty layer until it consumed everything.

He thought of the two women whose lives had ended in useless terror. Whose bodies now lay rigid on a cold slab in the morgue. *What a waste.* If he were a superstitious man, he'd wonder if it was more than a coincidence that they'd found the second body the day after Halloween.

Brady entered and made a beeline for the coffeepot on a counter near Harmon's desk. "Glad someone brewed the Java," he said. "My wife doesn't know the world exists before nine. All this equal rights shit. I used to get breakfast until she got liberated."

"Same litany I've heard for months," Harmon said. "I don't really give a rat's ass."

"Want some?" Brady asked, obviously choosing to ignore Harmon's foul mood."

"Of course I want some." He propped an elbow on his desk to support his throbbing head. "If it's not too much trouble."

"No trouble, boss." Brady set a steaming mug on the desk. "Got a headache?"

"Yeah. This." Harmon shoved the file across the desk. "Why isn't anyone looking for those women?"

"Take it you got zip from Missing Persons." Brady sat on the edge of Harmon's desk. "Want me to talk to Jenkins in Vice again. Maybe he's picked up some street news."

"Go ahead."

After his partner left, Harmon stood, stretched, then walked around his little section of the office. Nobody paid him much attention. They were all too busy with their own latest headache.

Pausing by the side of his desk, he rubbed the back of his neck in a vain attempt to ease the tension. His head felt like an iron band was squeezing it. Leaning over, he reached for the bottle of aspirin in his desk drawer. He didn't need any more aspirin. What he needed was a murderer in custody.

He had a gut feeling that even if they could come up with a name for one of the women, that meager lead wouldn't amount to much. He doubted whether the killer had any contact with the victims before their fateful meeting. So they'd still be looking for an unknown quantity. A sick, unknown quantity.

Harmon thought the only real hope they had lay in the old house. Whoever had been living in that upstairs room had been around for a while. He was willing to gamble that the occupant was also the killer.

Picking up the note he'd jotted as a reminder to call Detective Hobkins, Harmon felt a twinge of envy. It had been a long time since he'd felt the staunch determination she possessed. He wondered if he'd ever feel it again, or if determination was another lost entity.

He shrugged and sat down. *Call Hobkins first then do philosophy.*

After Harmon's call, Barbara drummed a pencil end on the desk and considered her options. She could brave the Chief's wrath one more time. Go behind his back. Or just forget the whole thing. The last choice she dismissed immediately. Personal integrity wouldn't let her accept the second. She didn't really have a choice at all. Only a problem. How was she going to convince Broyles to let her go to Dallas? *There won't be any convincing if you don't get off your ass and try.*

Resolute, she stood and walked down the hall to his office. She had two things in her favor. He was speaking to her again ,and Keith had wrapped up the burglary case.

Broyles frowned when he looked up and saw her. "What is it?"

"I need a couple of hours to go to Dallas this afternoon. Harmon wants me to consult on a case."

"Another psychotic killer?" His voice was tinged with sarcasm.

"Maybe." She refused to take his bait.

"Sorry. That crack was out of line." He leaned his elbows on the desk and rested his chin in his hands. "Just ran into a snag here. Shouldn't take it out on you."

"What happened?" Barbara sat in the chair across from him.

"That eyewitness couldn't positively ID Wertco in the lineup."

"Oh." She leaned forward.

"Don't leap to the wrong conclusion. It's just one small setback. We're not ready to throw the case out."

"Okay. Won't say a word." She smiled. "How about my request?"

"What about your caseload."

"Clear. Keith wrapped the Hansen burglary this morning. Turned out to be their ex-gardener. They fired him last month, and he decided to collect his own brand of severance pay."

Broyles made a dismissive gesture. "Just for this afternoon."

"You got it." She stood quickly. "And thanks."

"I owed you. For the other day."

Barbara smiled as she walked out. That was as close to an apology as the Chief could get. But she understood. Without formal education, he'd come up through the ranks as a tough guy. It was hard for him to break character.

She still remembered how intimidated she used to be around him. When she'd first joined the force she wouldn't dare to stand up to him. But she'd soon learned that if she wanted a share of the action, she had to push. After the first time it got easier.

She stopped by her office to get her jacket and pick up her notebook with the address Harmon had given her.

The early afternoon traffic was light on the interstate. Barbara set her cruise control at seventy-three and inserted a Pink Floyd CD. She'd discovered in college that loud noise helped her think. And she had a lot of thinking to do, especially about the snag Broyles had mentioned. She knew it wasn't enough to free the kid, but it was the first glimmer of hope in a week.

Arriving on the fringe of the downtown district a few minutes early, Barbara sat in her car studying the ancient Victorian house. It seemed to glare back at her with an air of haughty arrogance. In its day, it had probably been quite stunning. A graceful veranda swept across the front and down the right side. Barbara could almost picture a cluster of genteel ladies having afternoon tea on a white wicker table, a maid attending to every need. It was an image hard to hang onto as Barbara did a visual sweep of the rest of the house.

Huge, gnarled oaks framed the entire west side, as if protecting it from intrusion. A small, lopsided balcony under one of the upstairs windows gave the impression of an ominous Cyclops, all seeing, forever alert.

A slight shudder, not unlike the one produced by the Avery house, shook her. Grandmother Hobkins had said such sensations were caused by someone walking across a grave. A picture of the still fresh graves of Susan Delgrave and Aimee Nelson flashed through her mind.

How stupid. Comparing houses and graves and shudders. She was going from bad to worse, her thoughts a gory kaleidoscope of doubts, fears, and frustration.

Barbara watched in the rearview mirror as Harmon stopped his white Ford behind her. She waved as she got out of her car. "Howdy."

"Come on. Our forensic crew is finished now."

He led the way through the empty ground floor, up the staircase, and into the grisly murder scene. Despite the open windows, the air felt heavy, defying her lungs to work. The putrescent odor of death was unmistakable, and her breath caught in her throat. She placed a hand over her nose and mouth. "Hate to think of how bad it was yesterday."

"Couldn't eat the rest of the day." He spoke through fingers across his mouth. "Gets better after a few minutes, though."

"Was the body up here?"

"Yeah. Looked like the set for a slasher movie. Must've been here for three or four days. She was on an old blanket. At least what was left of her. Looks like the killer was probably waiting for a chance to wrap the body and dump it somewhere. Maybe the lake again."

"You've definitely tied it to the other Jane Doe?"

"Looks good. Rope's the same. Cause of death. Due to the condition of the lake body, it's hard to match the mutilations. But as far as I'm concerned, it's the same guy."

"I wonder..." Barbara thought for a moment. "Could I take a look at the blanket and rope?"

"Sure. Not much else around here. And we can damn sure find a better smelling place to talk."

Barbara followed Harmon to the Dallas station and kept her car windows down the whole way. Even the invisible fog of city exhaust smelled better than that house.

She felt a prickle of excitement when she saw the victim's shroud, earlier referred to by Harmon as a blanket. "I'll be damned," she said, turning the plastic-wrapped package over. "This is a quilt."

"Yes?"

"We had quilts at our crime scenes, too. What if it's the same guy?"

Harmon frowned. "I don't follow."

"Psychotic killers aren't always Boston stranglers, following the same exact pattern. So our guy has one thing against prostitutes and something else against my victims."

"That may be a stretch. I'm not even sure my vics were hookers."

"Sure. But what else do either one of us have?"

Harmon shrugged and sat on the edge of his desk.

"What's your next move?" Barbara asked.

"Depends on the lab report. Or if we get a lead from Vice. If it's a zero, we'll let the place cool off for a while. Then try a stake out."

"Let me know when your people finish with this." She pointed to the quilt. "I'd like to run a comparison."

"Maybe you can have it now." Harmon picked up a grimy, beige telephone.

Barbara looked around the office, noticing an aging morale poster held to the wall by cracking yellowed tape. The poster depicted a smiling uniformed officer with the caption: THIS IS YOUR POLICE FORCE. WEAR YOUR BADGE WITH PRIDE. Smiling, she wondered where all the pride had disappeared to. She hadn't felt much lately. Maybe it was all part of the hardening process Keith kept reminding her about.

"You can take it." Harmon's voice broke into her thoughts. "Just sign a receipt"

He slipped the package into another larger plastic bag and grinned. "Smells bad enough to be worth something, huh?"

"Has your pervert shown any interest in underwear?"

"Nothing at the crime scene. Why?"

Briefly, she told him about the locker room mischief and the unidentified underwear in her apartment, then she shrugged. "Guess I was hoping for another connection."

"Nope." Harmon grinned. "My guy likes them naked."

Barbara returned his smile halfheartedly then took the bag and left. Somehow she felt cheated. She didn't know what she'd expected. Maybe a note saying, "Hello there, I'm the big break you've been looking for."

She laughed at the thought. Talk about desperation.

All she had was the quilt. Quilt number three. Wasn't that something? Despite her initial excitement at seeing it, the logical part of her mind told her it might not be important. Lots of people save old quilts, which is exactly what the Chief had told her. All respect aside, he'd explode if she walked in with nothing more than another slim possibility.

But this was the only angle she had, so maybe she'd be better of pursuing it and stop trying to make something out of the panties.

Quickly she planned her moves. It would be smarter to get the comparison tests and leave the Chief out of it, especially since they hadn't made any connection between the two they had. If only the first one hadn't belonged to the victim.

Another 'if' thrown in the net for good measure. *Oh, hell. I've gone this far. Might as well go all the way. Take the quilt straight to Crowder.*

The forensic science lab was housed inside a modern new building on Twin Lakes' affluent north side. Future plans called for the detective and juvenile divisions to share the adjoining five acres, but those plans had been postponed yearly since Barbara first joined the force.

A lanky, Hispanic man guided a large buffer back and forth across the wide hall. He noticed Barbara and smiled a greeting, a flash of white teeth under the dark bush of his mustache. She acknowledged with a wave, then stepped over the black, coiled cord, her footsteps muffled by the buffer's wheeze.

She didn't look forward to seeing Crowder. The officers referred to him as 'the mad scientist' with good cause. His morbid personality and quick temper could, and did, intimidate even the most stalwart. Barbara had always been amused by the similarity of eccentricity between Crowder and Davies. Maybe being bizarre was a job requirement.

She found the specialist hunched over a microscope, apparently alone in the lab. She mentally braced herself for whatever part he chose to play today.

An exceptional forensic scientist and definitely over-qualified for Twin Lakes, he was biding his time. His abrasive personality had cost him his last job somewhere up north, but he was currently bucking for a position in New York. At least that's what she'd heard.

His size and appearance did nothing to endear him. A small man, barely over five feet, he'd been born with a cleft palate. His lips were thick with scars from several surgeries. What little hair he had was clumped like fur on a dog with severe mange, and the thick lenses of his glasses turned his small eyes into mere pinpricks.

Barbara had heard rumors that the DA hesitated to put Crowder on the stand because he didn't have a good courtroom presence, but she didn't care what he looked like. He was a wizard with a microscope, and his efforts had been a turning point in many of her cases.

"Suppose you want top priority on this." Crowder pushed his glasses up to the bridge of his narrow nose, where they rested for only a moment before sliding down again.

When she didn't reply, he continued his tirade. "You think I'm a goddam miracle worker? I got more work stacked up here than ten men could do in a month. And everyone wants results yesterday."

"No big rush." Barbara said.

He looked at her with a suspicious squint then adjusted the microscope and peered through the oculars again. "I hope not. I don't think you use half the stuff you bring in here, anyway."

Relieved that he hadn't asked for authorization for the tests, Barbara stepped back to the door. She wanted to escape before he launched one of his lectures on bureaucracy. "Just fit it in when you can," she said with a hand on the door. "And let me know when you've got something."

The Pink Lady wasn't sporting a very large crowd, and Yance Cleary was disappointed. Once he'd recovered from his initial disappointment over losing the Simpson deal, he'd been delighted with the attention he'd received after finding that body. Usually, the most exciting thing that ever happened, other than the occasional fight, was betting on how many drinks old Betron could polish off before slipping off the bar stool. Now, Cleary was bursting with eagerness to tell his story, down to the finest detail, and nobody would listen.

There was one couple hunched together in a corner booth, but the only time they came up for air was to poke another quarter in the jukebox. Or to wave to Cleary for another round. The two guys at the bar were equally disinterested. They were intent on a private conversation, leaning so close together he'd wondered at first if they were fruitcakes. He hated it when queers came in. Made the rest of the customers uncomfortable, and Cleary figured they should stick to their own joints.

Cleary was trying to figure a way to eavesdrop on their conversation when the door opened to admit another customer. A big grin spread across his puffy face. Here was someone who would listen. Anytime this guy came in he was interested in anything connected to the police.

As the man eased onto a barstool, Cleary moved toward him, shifting his weight to the balls of his feet. "The usual?"

The man nodded.

Cleary drew a beer in a frosty mug and set it on the bar. "Missed all the excitement the other day." he said, mopping a few drops of water from the wood.

The man regarded him with expressionless eyes. But he didn't tell him to fuck off, so Cleary figured it was okay to hang around. "Some whore got herself knocked off. I found her. Right in my building."

He paused to give the man the opportunity to show how impressed he was, but all Cleary got was the stare. But the guy was still listening. "Can you imagine?" he continued. "Some weirdo's been doin' God knows what up there, and I didn't even know it."

Something cold and hard passed through the man's eyes as Cleary talked, but he ignored it. He was too afraid of losing his captive audience if he stopped again. Even the two guys down the bar had paused to listen.

The man remained silent as Cleary related the rest of the story of calling the police and being a star witness. He embellished the telling with details that made him sound like a cross between Superman and God Almighty. Didn't matter. Who'd bother to check?

When he had to pause to answer the phone, the man laid down enough money for his beer and walked toward the door.

"Hey, thanks a lot, fucker." Cleary said, hanging up. "Could at least stay to hear the end."

The guys at the bar laughed.

His mind whirled. Why was everything falling apart? It wasn't fair. Now he couldn't go back. Son of a bitch! What was he going to do?

Maybe it wasn't really so bad. He could stay away until the heat died down. Maybe—

Stop it! He grabbed his head in his powerful hands and tried to control the endless hacking of his thoughts. He couldn't stand it if he could never go back.

Maybe that cop had something to do with it. He should've finished her off before. Tried harder. But it wasn't his fault other people kept getting in the way.

Besides, he didn't really want to just finish her off. No satisfaction in that. The momentary surge as the life was squeezed out, then nothing. There could be more, lots more to be enjoyed.

A delicious thrill came with the game. Hunting. Stalking, like a wolf in the shadows until fear paralyzed the prey. Then the swift move that finalized the game.

Yes, that's how it should be. Even as he considered it, he felt his anxiety ebb away. He could think clearly again. He didn't have to rush into anything.

He'd stay away from his place as long as he had to. And in the meantime...

Chapter Twenty

Wednesday, November 3—Twin Lakes

It was another warm, almost summery afternoon. The sun blazed across a blue sky so bright it was almost painful to look at. A light breeze lifted the curtain at Barbara's kitchen window, bringing with it an invigorating smell of outdoor freshness.

She gazed through the smudged glass and, for a moment, wished she could be a child again. It would be so nice to desert responsibility: run and play in the cool security of the woods behind her parent's house. Maturity acted as a thief. Not only did it steal time, it also stole the wild abandonment of childhood.

My heavy thought for the day. She laughed and rubbed the top of Charlotte's head.

Philosophy was a pleasant change of pace from the niggling little fears that had been growing with each minute, hour, and day that passed. She tried to tell herself the last threat was meaningless, but the words had little impact on the feelings.

Even though no unwanted visitor invaded her apartment recently, she felt at times as if unknown eyes were on her. Like the incident at the taco stand. Nothing tangible, but...

This was her first day off in over a week, and she was trying to enjoy it. But she couldn't stop thinking about the case. *Why doesn't Crowder hurry up and call? End this nightmare.*

A quest for patience had become a high priority with Barbara. So, why was she sitting here impatiently waiting for the report? She knew better than to expect a call today. Even if the old bastard had nothing else to do, he'd put her off until Monday at the earliest.

"I've got to get out of here," she said to the cat. "I'm getting as wacko as old Crowder."

She went into the bedroom and selected a new blazer, a deep, rich hunter green, and her black slacks. She hadn't decided where to go, but anywhere would be better than here. She thought of her parents. *It's been weeks since I've seen them.* Any day now, she expected to get one of her mother's curt little reminders in the mail:

Dear Ms. Hobkins,
Your parents are alive and well. Hope you are the same.

She smiled. What her mother lacked in subtlety, she more than made up for in love.

The phone rang just when she was ready to walk out the door. She hurried back to answer. "Hello?"

"How'd you like to run away for the day?"

Barbara found Gene's question intriguing. "Depends on what you have in mind. A girl does have a reputation to uphold."

"My intentions are completely honorable."

His suggestion that they drive into Dallas and spend some time at the Galleria Mall sounded good. It would be easier for her to keep her mind off the job in crowds of people. And he had no problem with stopping by her folk's house on the way back.

They'd been at the mall for over an hour and, for some reason, Barbara felt remote, like a part of her was detached from the bustle of other shoppers. Several times, she caught herself only half listening to Gene.

Watching the young people drift through the mall in small groups, joking and laughing, Barbara couldn't help but think of Royce. He'd always been on the fringe of all that is normal in adolescence. Things could've been so different for him... if only... Another 'if.' Instead, he spent half his teenage years in reform school and stood to lose the rest of his life on a murder-one charge.

"Why do I feel like I'm alone?" Gene whispered in her ear.

"Sorry." She could feel the warmth of a flush spread across her cheeks.

"You've been somewhere else all afternoon. Something wrong?"

Barbara didn't answer. She wanted to tell him everything: the doubts, the fears. She wanted to ask him all the questions she struggled with. But, there were some professional boundaries involved."Come on," he said. "Let's get some coffee."

He led her down the walkway to a little English pub tucked between a shoe store and a beauty shop. After they were seated and placed their order, he leaned back on the padded, red leather. "Want to talk about it?"

"It's difficult." Barbara hesitated while the waitress set two steaming mugs on the table. "Professional restrictions."

"Then it *is* about the case?"

Barbara nodded, mentally sorting what she could say to him and what she couldn't. She took a sip of the French Roast then looked at him. "I'm not sure we've got the right guy locked up."

"You may be right."

Interesting, Barbara thought. The rest she said aloud. "Why do you say that?"

"I don't know what your evidence is, but I know that kid." He stirred cream and sugar into his cup, then continued. "A model student, he isn't. And, I'm glad

I don't have a whole school full of kids like him. But I don't think he could kill anybody."

Barbara sipped her coffee and regarded him over the rim of the cup. What he said made her feel better than she had in weeks.

"Didn't mean to put you in a bind. Bringing this up, I mean."

"That's okay." She set her cup down. "I can't discuss the evidence going to the Grand Jury. But I can tell you about another possibility."

She gave him a quick version of her visit to Dallas and the possibility of the quilt tie-in.

"You think the same guy killed Susan and Aimee?"

"Possibly."

"But how can you prove it with the quilt? Wasn't that Tom and Susan's at..." His voice faltered, and she touched his hand.

"All I'm hoping for at this point is a break in the case against Royce," she said. "That will open the investigation again."

During the drive to her parent's house in Garland, Gene was quiet, but it wasn't an uneasy silence. Barbara was content to watch the activities of the outside world as they rolled by: kids playing soccer on a field carpeted with brown grass, a white-haired lady walking her apricot poodle, a young couple raking leaves into a Technicolor pile.

The scenes held some appeal. It would be nice to just enjoy a glorious afternoon, but she knew she'd soon tire of the ordinariness of it. People like her didn't do well with ordinary.

She had to laugh at the thought. *That's why you mess up your life pretty regularly.*

Barbara led the way up the front walk to the small slab of concrete that doubled for a porch at her parents' brick home. "We don't have to stay long," she said to Gene who trailed a step behind. "Mother will probably jump to all the wrong conclusions."

"And what might those be?"

Punching the doorbell, she gave him a sidelong look. "It's been a while since I've brought anybody with me."

Whatever he might have wanted to say in response was interrupted as the door opened.

"Hi, Mom. This is Gene Wilkins." Barbara stepped into the house and he followed.

"Do I call you Mom, too?" Gene reached out to shake her hand.

"I'm Ethel."

Barbara groaned when she saw the sparkle in her mother's eyes. Then the older woman smiled at Gene, touched the perfect wave in her platinum hair, then smiled again. "Harold," she called. "Look who's here."

When her father came out of the living room, he at least had the good sense to act normal. After introductions were made, he led Gene back to the living room. Her mother hustled Barbara toward the large, country-style kitchen to help make coffee. *As if she ever needed help.*

"What a nice young man," Ethel said, assembling delicate cups on a silver tray. "You didn't tell me you met someone else."

"This is our second date mom. Don't let your mind go where I think it's going."

"I'm not thinking anything."

The comment was so absurd that Barbara laughed, then her mother joined in.

"I know you all too well," Barbara said. "Don't be calling the preacher yet."

"I just think a woman needs a man in her life."

"Yes, mom, you're right. But don't let your need for grandchildren cloud your good sense." She picked up the tray and turned to the door. "Let's go before daddy scares him away."

During the rest of the visit, Barbara smothered her smiles when her mother was a bit obvious with her questions. But Gene handled it deftly. She was tempted to accept her mother's invitation to dinner, but decided two hours fulfilled the requisite visiting time. Didn't want to spoil her chances with the man because of a pushy mother.

"I like your parents," Gene said as they pulled out of the driveway.

"Thanks."

Barbara settled back in the seat. He was happy. Her mother was happy. And Barbara realized she was happy. *All in all, not a bad afternoon.*

"How about coming up?" she asked when they pulled in front of her apartment complex. "I could scrounge up something to eat."

"That'd be great."

Charlotte greeted them at the door. She wasn't friendly toward Gene, but she didn't run and hide either. *Another litmus test passed successfully.*

Make yourself at home," Barbara said before heading into the kitchen.

Gene threw his jacket over the back of the pale blue sofa and scratched the cat under the chin when she jumped up to investigate. Then he followed Barbara into the kitchen.

"I've got some eggs," she said. "How about scrambled with sausage?"

"Can I help?"

"This is strictly a one-person kitchen. Even Charlotte crowds me sometimes."

Gene leaned on the doorframe and watched Barbara move through an efficient routine of browning the meat, whisking the eggs, and setting out plates. She didn't waste a minute or a move.

After she poured the egg mixture into the skillet, she glanced at him. "Would you mind terribly getting my mail? I forgot."

"No problem."

He returned a few minutes later with a handful of odd sized envelopes and flyers.

"Anything good?" Barbara asked.

"Isn't there some law about looking at someone else's mail?"

"No, just opening it."

Gene laughed and quickly sorted through the items. "Looks like 'occupant' hit a bonanza. "Resident' is a close second. Oh, here's something actually addressed to you by name."

He dropped a thick envelope on the counter. Barbara glanced over then sucked in a quick breath. She dropped the spatula and slowly wiped her hands on a towel before reaching for the envelope. The scrawl of the handwriting was all too familiar.

"Something the matter?" Gene asked.

"I don't know." She picked up a butter knife from the counter and slipped it inside the flap. "Looks like an instant replay of a crank letter I got."

Careful about how she handled it, Barbara pulled out a single sheet of paper and unfolded it. A small plastic bag fell on the counter with a dull plop. Momentarily forgetting the note, she used her tongs to pick up the bag.

Gene leaned toward her. "What is it?"

"I'm not sure." Barbara stared at the pale, colorless thing in the bottom of the bag. Even without touching it, she knew it would be soft. It would yield to pressure. Clenching her teeth, she forced down the sick churning in her stomach. "Looks like a piece of rotten meat."

"Who on earth would-"

She cut him off with a wave of her hand and opened the note. She held it flat to the counter with the edge of the knife and read the message:

Time is gone. Don't you know?

Roses bleed red. Dead. Dead. Dead.

The words didn't make sense. They didn't have to. They were like a living, breathing threat leaping off the page.

Something pushed at Barbara's consciousness, something that could be of vital importance. If this wasn't another crank, it could be a turning point for Royce. He couldn't have sent this one. He'd been in custody for over a week.

"Sorry to renege on dinner," she said, motioning to Gene. "But I've got to get this to the lab."

Gene watched her car disappear around the corner then slid into the driver's seat of his own. It all happened so fast, he didn't even have a chance to say anything: tell her he was worried, ask her to be careful.

He didn't expect the intensity of feelings she aroused. He told himself he wasn't going to feel this way again. This all started as a personal challenge. *How close can I get without risking?*

But the sight of that meat in the Baggie... And the threatening words... They'd hit him hard, and he recognized the signs of caring. Whether this was good for him or not, he didn't know. He just knew he wanted to watch over her. It would be like it was with Nancy those first years when things were so good between them.

Chapter Twenty-One

Monday, November 8—Twin Lakes

Punching his thin, musty pillow in frustration, Royce propped it under his head and stretched out on the lumpy mattress of the cot. Sleep had been an unattainable luxury the past few days. Not because of the obvious lack of creature comforts afforded by the county jail, but because of the desperation that kept picking away at him like a relentless buzzard.

Without a watch, he had no idea what time it was, but his inner clock told him it was probably early morning. In a few hours, the Grand Jury would be meeting to decide his fate, and no matter how hard he tried, Royce couldn't resign himself to it. His lawyer, anticipating the decision would be unfavorable, was pushing to cop a plea.

Isn't this a bitch? I've been talking my way out of trouble since I was ten. Now I can't talk, or even beg, my way out of something I didn't do.

For the first time in his life, Royce felt a pure, cold stab of fear. It was like he was perched at the top of a roller coaster hill in a car he knew would derail halfway down.

If only that damn cop hadn't dangled a small ray of hope. He knew better than to believe she would help. She didn't bail him out of anything three years ago, and she sure as hell wasn't going to do it now. *That's what you get for trusting a cop, Royce, baby. Shit on your head. She probably didn't even try.*

Rolling over, he did something he hadn't done in years. He buried his head in his pillow and cried like a baby.

The pair of massive, carved oak doors of the central jury room dominated the corridor of the old County Courthouse. Each time Barbara passed them in her endless pacing, she hesitated briefly as if this might be the time she'd be allowed to penetrate the heavy wood and become party to the proceedings. This was the first day of testimony, and no one expected it to take very long.

Where the hell is that lab report?

When a door opened further down the hall, she whirled, hoping, but Keith shook his head.

"Damn!" she said. "What's keeping them?"

"You know Crowder. He won't do anything out of order. Said he'd get to it this morning." Keith leaned against the wall and crossed his arms, pulling the fabric of his gray serge suit coat tight across his shoulders. "You been called yet?"

"I think the Chief arranged it so I wouldn't. Doesn't want me and my wild-ass ideas in there."

"You're being a little rough on him, don't you think?"

"Chalk it up to paranoia." Barbara started to walk away, then changed her mind. "Got a cigarette?"

"You don't smoke."

"Chewed all my fingernails."

"I refuse to be an accessory to the beginning of another nasty habit."

She laughed, then glanced at the big clock on the wall. "Is it only ten? It feels like I've been here forever."

Keith wandered down the hall, studying the framed photographs of the honorable judges who'd graced the court through the years. Barbara wished she could disassociate so easily.

Finally, she couldn't stand it anymore. "Would you call Crowder again?"

Keith looked at her in mock horror. "You nuts?"

"Please?"

"Don't 'Please' me. I'd do almost anything for you. But Crowder? No way. I'm still stinging from the last time I got in his hair."

Another hour ticked slowly around the clock. Keith brought Barbara her third cup of coffee and they continued their vigil.

"I'm going to call," she said. "Surely he has the report by now."

He shook his head. "Good luck."

Crowder came on the line almost immediately after Barbara identified herself. Before she got another word out, his loud voice assailed her through the receiver. "This sample you brought in. 'Top priority' you said. 'It's important' you said." Momentarily, Crowder choked on his anger. "Important, my ass!"

"What is it?"

He ignored her. "Seven-thirty this morning I was ready to handle your project. And what did I find? I'll tell you what I found. Pigskin."

"Pigskin?" Barbara's voice was as loud as his.

"Are we playing a game here? I said pigskin and that's what I meant."

Her heart sank. She searched for words that might soothe Crowder's anger. "Sorry. Guess I was taken in by some kind of crank. I'm sure it..."

She heard the dull buzz of a dial tone and slowly hung up. She turned to Keith. "You heard?"

He nodded. "Want me to tell the Chief?"

"He didn't want to hear about it unless it was, and I quote, 'pertinent.' Besides, I'm sure Crowder will file a full report."

"Hell. It's not your fault the stuff came from Porky." Keith paused, looking for something positive to say. "Maybe we'll get a break on the quilt."

He looked so hopeful, Barbara had to smile. "Yeah. Maybe."

An hour later, the courtroom doors opened, and a jubilant DA Harrison walked out. His smile lit up his mahogany face, and he tugged at the lapel of his dark pinstripe suit. He glanced over at Barbara and Keith. "Murder One," he said.

Damn. Barbara turned away and strode out of the building. *Nothing left to do today but go home.*

After changing into a pair of gray sweats, she fixed a cheerless frozen dinner and thought about what to do this evening. No way did she want to stay home and feel beaten. She thought about calling Gene, even started to dial his number then stopped. Her life had been consumed with the case or her love life for too long. *Maybe it's time to take a break from both.*

She dialed Marcy's number. It'd been ages since they'd gone to a movie together. The machine answered after the third ring, and Barbara exhaled her frustration in a long sigh.

Charlotte jumped on the counter and investigated the remnants of macaroni in an aluminum dish. Only when the dish was dangerously near the edge, did Barbara realize what was going on. Absently, she reached out and held it in place. "Someday I'm going to have to teach you some manners."

The cat gazed at her with wide amber eyes before resuming the task at hand.

"Looks like it's just me and you." She scratched Charlotte's ear. Almost immediately, a soft rumble vibrated against Barbara's fingers.

Walking into the living room with the cat in her arms, she was suddenly alert to the faint sound of scraping on the other side of the door. Tightening her grip on the cat, Barbara held her breath, straining to hear more.

Nothing.

The cat objected to her grip by pushing out of her arms. Barbara let her go, with her gaze still glued to the door. *Had the knob moved or was it just her imagination?*

"Who's there?"

When the stupidity of the question hit her, Barbara almost laughed. She never realized that fear had the capacity to reduce a person to such idiocy.

The simple act of acknowledging her own weakness gave her a chance to regroup mentally and let her training take over. Her holster, with the gun still in it, was right there on the library table. Slipping the weapon out, she checked it and moved quietly to the door. She listened for a moment then threw the door open.

Whatever she expected, it wasn't the sight of Mr. Gilroy bent over his lock across the hall. He turned. "Good evening Miss, Hobkins." His gaze hovered on the weapon in her hand. "Looking for one of your criminals?"

She lowered the gun. "Sorry. I heard... Did you see anyone in the hall when you came up?"

"No." He continued to focus on the gun.

"Guess its just nerves." She tucked the weapon behind her back. "Didn't mean to scare you."

He gave her a brief wave before disappearing into his apartment. Barbara quickly closed and locked her door, leaning her back against the solid feel of wood.

When the buzzer went off next to her ear, a rush of adrenaline sent her heart thundering in her chest. She took a second to steady her breathing, then pressed the button. "Yes?"

"It's me. Can I come up?"

Recognizing Keith's voice, she deactivated the downstairs lock, then stowed her gun. If he saw her brandishing it, he'd think she was nuts for sure.

A loud rap sounded on her door, and she opened it to let him in. The tight lines around his mouth indicated this was not a social visit. "What's wrong?" she asked.

He took a moment to look her over. "I could ask you the same question."

She shrugged. "Just a little spooked."

A quick glance at his face told her he wasn't buying it. Hoping a diversion would work, she headed toward the kitchen. "Want some coffee?"

"Maybe you better look at this first."

A tone in his voice made her stop and look back at him. He was still in the middle of the room, brows knit together, and his coat still on. That's when she noticed the brown file folder in his hand.

"What's that?" She walked toward him.

He held it out. "Just read it."

Disturbed by his curt manner, she opened the folder and pulled out a Missing Person's report. Sinking to the couch, Barbara started to scan the page, then her attention riveted on the name: Nancy Wilkins. *What? I thought they were divorced!*

She continued to read. Some details found clarity in the mad swirl of her mind. 'Subject reported missing two days before court hearing.' 'Husband filed report.' 'No indication of foul play.'

When the inner turmoil threatened to boil over, she looked at Keith. "You ran a check on him?"

"Yeah. Figured you should know what you're getting into."

"You're worried because his wife disappeared? Lots of people do a walk-away."

"Has he told you all this?" Keith gestured vaguely to the papers still clutched in her hand.

"That doesn't mean anything." Barbara stood and leaned into him. "Would you share your deepest pain if you lost Brenda?"

"It's not the same thing."

"Think about it Keith. When someone walks out of your life like that, it's damn personal."

He dug a toe into the short pile of the carpeting, then he glanced at her. "Do what you want. I was just giving you a head's up."

Anger churned as Barbara watched him turn and walk out of her apartment. But she wasn't sure to whom she should direct the anger. Gene for not being honest with her, or Keith for slapping her in the face with it.

Shit! She didn't need this new complication. Not when her nerves were already so jangled she felt like a poorly constructed marionette, ready to fall apart at any moment.

But she knew she couldn't just ignore it because it wasn't convenient. She checked her watch. Nine-forty. A little late, but she might as well go before she talked herself out of it.

Gene opened the door, surprised to see Barbara standing there.

"We need to talk," she said, brushing past him.

What the hell? He followed her to the living room, taking note of her casual attire and stiff-legged walk. When she turned to face him, her expression was grim. "Tell me about your wife."

"Wha..." He ran a hand across his mouth. "Why don't you sit down."

Barbara stood in the middle of the room, arms crossed across her chest. "I thought you said you were divorced."

"I never said that."

"It's what you led me to believe."

She watched him cast his gaze around the room, looking anywhere but at her.

"I don't want to talk about this."

His words were hard, final, closing a door. Barbara took a step toward him. "What happened, Gene?"

"She's gone." He looked at her now. "That's enough, isn't it?"

Defiance dominated his eyes, but Barbara could see a flicker of pain. "Why didn't you tell me from the start?"

"Because it's done. Over." He walked away from her and leaned against the mantle. "It doesn't matter any more."

She studied his rigid back for a moment. "It matters if it still hurts."

The silence seemed ready to explode, and Barbara wasn't quite sure what to do. If she went to him, touched him, would he burst?

Finally he spoke, each word so soft, she had to lean forward to hear him. "Her parents were sure I did something to drive her away. They couldn't understand that she... just left." He took a deep breath. "How can I put words to the humiliation?"

This time the silence overflowed with pain. Barbara walked over and stood behind him, still not sure about touching him. "Gene, I'm sorry."

He kept his face averted. "You better go now."

She took a step back and looked at him. He stood rigid and unyielding.

"You understand why I had to know?" she asked.

He didn't answer.

Back at her apartment, Barbara closed the door, threw the deadbolt then leaned against the cool wood, her breath coming in harsh gasps. *What a night.*

Her earlier fear had returned the minute she entered the building and sent her racing up the stairs. Now, she didn't know what to be most afraid of. That some intruder might bust through the door, or that it might be over with Gene.

She pulled herself away from the security of something solid at her back and headed toward the bedroom. Somehow she had to stop the swirl of emotions before the storm scuttled what little control she had left. She could still see Gene poised in front of his fireplace, his cold reserve a more effective barrier than a steel wall between them. Would things ever be the same again? Did she want them to be? *Questions. Questions. Questions, and who the hell has an answer?*

Turning on the shower, she stripped, dropping her clothes in the middle of the floor, then stepped into the steam. She tried to surrender to the calming effect of hot water rushing across her body, and it almost worked. Until she got in bed. Then her mind went into high gear again. She threw the covers back and padded into the kitchen. A few minutes of digging in the cabinet over her sink unearthed a dusty bottle of scotch. It wasn't her drink of choice. She'd bought it for Roger. *But what the hell, he'll never be back to drink it. And it'll knock me out.*

Even so, sleep didn't come easily. When it did, it was light and fitful. Every time the cat moved, the rustle brought Barbara fully awake, and she lay listening to the night noises before drifting into sleep again. A full hour before her alarm was due to go off, she awoke to the sounds of crying. Dazed from sleep, she put her hands to her own wet cheeks. The dream remained startlingly clear...

Coming in the apartment to find Charlotte sitting in the hallway, Barbara reaches down to stroke her. At the touch of her fingers, the cat's head topples and rolls crazily across the light carpeting. She backs away from the wide amber eyes staring up at her. Then she hears a harsh voice from her bedroom. "We're here Barbara."

She races toward the sound. Her bedroom door is closed, the knob coated with a slick, amber substance making it impossible to turn. She smears the goo on the wall and tries again. The knob continues to slip beneath her fingers. The voices are still there, calling her, "Come to the party, Barbara."

Suddenly the door gives and Barbara stumbles in, her momentum almost taking her to her knees.. Then she freezes, staring in horror at monstrous specters of Susan Delgrave and Aimee Nelson. They are little more than skeletons, with rotting, putrid skin clinging to exposed bone. Fingers white as ivory clutch the corners of a faded quilt and raise it above their heads. Then they slowly lower the quilt atop dozens of others already on the bed. Ignoring Barbara, they repeat the actions until the bed sags under a tremendous weight.

"We're ready now." Susan Delgrave turns to face Barbara, a twisted smile on her torn, bloody face.

"Noooo." Barbara screams as they rush toward her.

Those horrible hands grab her and drag her toward the bed. The last thing she hears, as the weight of another quilt crushes her into darkness, is a male voice coming from above. "It's time to tuck you in."

Bolting upright, Barbara clutched the blanket to her chin and sat trembling until fingers of dawn touched the patch of sky she could see from her window.

Chapter Twenty-Two

Tuesday, November 9—Twin Lakes

Keith looked up in surprise when one of the lab assistants walked into the office with a report for Barbara. This can't be something for a new case. They weren't reassigned yet.

Curiosity overcame courtesy. He put his coffee down and pulled the folder across to his desk. From the tone of the message inside, Crowder was still stinging from the last request from Detective Hobkins. Keith smiled. *She sure has a way of stirring the ire of even the most patient of people.*

He read the information again, trying to figure what it was about. It was a preliminary report on some fabric comparisons. *But what the hell for?* Then he remembered Barbara's obsession with the quilts. *Is she still digging into that? Officially? Will she talk to me about it or freeze me out because of last night?*

"Crowder's man just delivered this." Keith threw the report on her desk when Barbara walked in. She glanced quickly at the folder.

Other than the puffy darkness under her eyes, she looked okay. Not an icicle in sight. "What gives?" he asked.

Her explanation was clipped: just the fact that Crowder was doing more fabric comparisons, but, at least, they'd jumped the hurdle of actually speaking to each other.

"The Chief's going to blow his stack," he said.

"Not really."

"How so?"

"He sort of gave me the go-ahead." She turned and hung up her coat.

Keith felt the last of his anxiety slip away. The talking came easier with each word. Now, it was almost like any other day.

"What did you do? Blackmail him?"

Barbara dismissed his question with a vague gesture and picked up the report. After reading it, she threw it down in disgust. "Damn! Damn! Damn!"

Keith regarded her outburst with mild amusement. "What did you expect?"

"Something to connect all the quilts to one person." She picked up the paper again and read aloud. "'Similarities of stitches and fabric except for Quilt A.' I knew that one wouldn't match. It's the Delgrave quilt. And the worst part is, he didn't check the dye lots."

"There's still time. Maybe something else will turn up."

"Right." Barbara stood and paced in the narrow confines of their office. "The killer's not going to wait for us to catch up to him."

Keith shrugged and turned back to the stack of papers on his desk. As far as he was concerned, he was delighted the Nelson case was wrapped up. He'd gone a whole week now without having to pop an antacid pill every thirty minutes. But, if he were completely honest, he'd admit that a small part of him was still uneasy. A few pieces still didn't fit without a good push, and he didn't like that approach. He liked his cases neat and clean, with no unanswered questions.

The shrill ring of his phone broke his chain of thoughts. He picked up the receiver and tucked it between his ear and shoulder. "Reeves." Looking up, he was surprised to see that, sometime in the last few minutes, Barbara had left.

Keith didn't recognize the gruff male voice asking for her, but something about it raised the hair on the back of his neck. It was like the voices in the monster movies that scared the piss out of him when he was a kid.

"Who's calling?" he asked.

Silence answered the question, followed a few seconds later by a click, then the line going dead.

Uneasiness crawled out of its deep recess and churned in his stomach. He shook his head. *Cool it. Don't let it start up again. The call might have nothing to do with the cases. Might even be that jerk she was thick with before.*

Keith was still trying to convince himself when the phone rang again. Swiftly, he scooped up the receiver. "Reeves."

Again, a strange male voice asked for his partner. But, this one wasn't so sinister.

"She's not here," Keith said. "Can I help you?"

The caller seemed unsure for a moment before identifying himself. The name got his full attention.

"Yes, Mr. Delgrave. Can I take a message?"

"It's about the quilt I identified that night..." Tom's voice cracked and he coughed. "It wasn't ours."

"Are you sure?"

"I got a call from the cleaners this morning. The man said they don't normally do anything about items left over thirty days. But he knew Susan and... Anyway, he said our quilt was still there. Susan took it in a few days before..."

"Why did he wait this long to call?"

"He thought I knew. Figured I'd come for it when I could."

Keith's mind went into high gear. *What if Barbara was right all along?* "Thanks for the information, Mr. Delgrave. We'll get back to you."

After he hung up, Keith realized he might be jumping to conclusions. The fact that the quilt didn't belong to the victim didn't necessarily change the case. If the kid took his own quilt to the Nelson scene, he could've done the same before.

Then again, it was another little piece that didn't fit. *Should they just keep pushing or make sure they had the right pieces?*

He considered waiting until Barbara came back, then decided against it. He didn't know where she went or when she'd be back. He jotted a quick note, propped it on her telephone, and went to find Chief Broyles.

In sheer frustration, Barbara had slipped away to find a place where she could make a private phone call. The only two people who shared her feelings about the case were Harmon and Gene. Since he couldn't help her with the investigation, she dialed the number for Dallas Central.

Barbara's short conversation with Harmon proved fruitful. The stakeout of the old house was set for Friday night, and Harmon said she could be there. Now, all she needed to do was convince the Chief to let her go. She squared her shoulders and headed to his office.

Keith's presence there and the excited expression he wore, diverted her momentarily. "What's up?"

He gave her the gist of the call from Delgrave.

"I knew it." Barbara leaned over Broyles' desk. "We thought the quilts didn't match because the first one belonged to the victim. Now that we know it didn't, why didn't we get a match?"

"Hold it." Broyles tilted back in his chair. "This doesn't change anything."

"Yes it does." Barbara grabbed a chair and straddled it, ticking items off on her fingers. "If we contend Royce did both murders and brought the quilts with him, there should be some similarities. The mother said her quilts all came from an aunt. We'd get some matches on fabric and thread." She paused for a breath, then finished in a flurry of words. "The DA and everyone seems to be content with hanging him on the Nelson murder. So, maybe he did do the girl. But no way on Delgrave."

"Hey, don't yell at me. I didn't bring in the indictment," Broyles said.

Barbara let out the breath in exasperation. "You know as well as I do that all we've got against the kid is a lot of circumstantial evidence."

Broyles rubbed his thumb across the stubble on his cheek, eyes narrowed. Barbara didn't know if he was considering her argument or getting ready to call her on insubordination.

Keith cleared his throat. "Can I say something?"

Broyles swiveled his chair until he faced the other man.

"For some dumb reason, I'm starting to think she's right." Keith raised a hand to stop the Chief's outburst. "I've ignored some of the loose ends because I was as anxious as everyone else to clear the cases. But it's not working. Maybe we owe it to ourselves to tie this up a little tighter."

"I'm up against the wall on this." Broyles sighed. "The commissioner's a blood sucker when it comes to money."

"How loud can he protest if we're gathering information to strengthen the case?" Barbara asked.

Broyles studied her for a moment. "Is that what you're doing?"

"I'm looking for evidence. Any evidence." She gripped the back of the chair. "Don't even *think* that I'm just on some personal crusade. If the kid really did it, I'll be happy to pull the switch."

Keith held his breath, waiting for an eruption from his boss, but Broyles sat like a statue. Then he sighed. "Okay," he said. "You want to bust your asses on your own, you've got until Monday."

He paused, waiting for nods of assent from both the detectives then faced Barbara again. "I'm only going to say this once. This is my department. You embarrass me on this and you'll be in the typing pool."

"Yes, sir." Barbara rose and, for one frightened moment, Broyles thought she was going to kiss him. Instead, she grabbed her purse and rushed out.

Keith threw the Chief a mock-salute and hurried after her.

Chapter Twenty-Three

Friday, November 12—Dallas

Harmon slowly cruised down Oak Lawn, where streetlights offered patches of illumination. Pedestrian traffic had abruptly thinned after his turn off Cedar Springs, and his hope rose. Without heavy congestion, it was easier to spot any-one going into or out of the old house, one small, positive note in a melody of negatives.

He couldn't remember the last time he felt so frustrated with a case. Every-where he turned, he ran into blank walls, an endless chain of blank walls. He was banking a lot on this stakeout. With a little bit of luck, the guy might walk right into their trap.

Pulling abreast of the house, he noted his man at the gas station across the street. It was a maneuver highly overdone in film, but, the hell of it was, it worked. At least it did in the movies.

At the next intersection, Harmon took a quick right and then right again on a street that took him behind the house. Away from the artificial light, he couldn't see anything on this moonless night. Tall, scruffy bushes flanked the back parking lot, but he knew when he passed it. The exact location was permanently etched in his mind.

About fifty yards beyond the rear of the house, a driveway led to a modern office building that looked grossly out of place. The whole area was made up of old structures dating back to the early 1900s, intermingled with post-war houses fallen to decay a long time ago. The new building looked like a Jaguar in the middle of a junkyard.

But Harmon was glad it was there. The structure was raised on huge pillars over a parking lot, and the southwest corner of the lot offered a clear view of the back of the old house.

Dousing his lights while he was still covered by the dense foliage to one side, Harmon stopped the car. A few seconds later, Brady appeared like a shadow out of the darkness.

"You're pretty good at this," Harmon said.

"Learned it from an old Indian scout," Brady said with a grin.

"Very funny. Any action yet?"

"Nope. Everything's nice and quiet. Me and J.C. are entertaining ourselves with old comedy routines."

"Don't get carried away and miss something. Hate to think you were laughing your ass off while I get all the glory."

"No sweat boss. We're with you all the way."

"I'm going to park somewhere over on Congress and wait. Simms is pumping gas like a pro, and Hobkins should be here any minute. If it's going to happen tonight, it'll probably be in the next few hours. Three beeps if we spot someone going in the house."

Brady nodded and faded silently into the shadows. Harmon waited a minute then backed out. He didn't turn on his lights until he was headed east on Shelby. He went the full block and a half to Cedar Springs and passed the house one more time. *Okay, baby. Cough up your pervert tonight. Right into Harmon's waiting arms.*

Checking his mirror, he noted a blue Datsun pulling into the gas station. He glanced at his watch. *Ten o'clock. She's right on time.*

Barbara slowed to the right of the pumps and stopped in front of the garage doors. For the next few hours, she'd appear to be just a lady waiting to get her car repaired. When Simms was ready, she pulled into the garage, where he would tinker with the engine between customers.

During the briefing, Barbara had found out that Simms didn't know an internal combustion engine from a sewing machine. She warned him to make sure her car was still running when she was ready to leave. He'd laughed and assured her that one thing he was exceptionally good at was appearing to be busy while doing nothing. "People driving by will think I'm Mr. Goodwrench himself, and I won't even have grease on my fingers."

After a long hour of waiting, Barbara heard a voice coming across the walkie-talkie. "Hobkins, you read?"

"Yes, Harmon."

"Subject making a third trip down the street. Average height and build, wearing a dark suit. You and Simms get a look. Could be our guy."

Barbara signed off and replaced the walkie-talkie in her canvas bag, then stepped out of the station. Simms was coming across the pitted asphalt with a credit card in his hand.

"We've got a possible across the street," Barbara said without looking directly at him.

The man Harmon described was walking east. Barbara watched until he reached the Melrose Hotel, where he paused as if deliberating about going in. Barbara moved to her left at the entrance of the garage. Traffic momentarily blocked her view, so she stepped to the far corner.

Simms took a position behind her. "Anything?"

"Not yet. He walked up and down Oak Lawn several times according to Harmon."

Barbara continued to watch the man silhouetted in the pale hotel lights. He rested for a moment on a low brick wall that flanked the walkway on both sides. He just sat there, pulling at the leaves on the bushes. *Why doesn't he move? Do something, damn you. Come back where I can get a good look at you.*

Finally, the man stood and headed back in Barbara's direction. There was something about his ambling walk, almost a shuffle, that tugged a familiar chord. She was almost certain she'd seen that peculiar gait before. As he approached the ring of illumination from the streetlight, she stepped out of the doorway to get a better look.

Suddenly, she was blinded when a car pulled into the station, bathing her in light as bright as a spot on center stage. "Damn it!" she said as the car swept past.

When she had a clear line of vision again, the sidewalk in front of the hotel was empty. Further down, she spotted a man rounding the corner. But she couldn't be sure it was the same guy.

Stepping up beside her, Simms gave her a questioning look. She shook her head and nodded toward the car now parked in front of the full-serve pump. "Might as well carry on," she said. "Our guy might still be out there watching."

Let it be so. She turned back into the garage. *Don't let the whole thing fall apart because some poor bastard needed gas.*

He mingled with the people drifting slowly up Cedar Springs. Still trembling, he ignored the greasy, red smiles and come-ons from the hookers leaning in doorways and against storefronts. *What the fuck was that bitch doing there?*

It was an unbelievable stroke of luck that he'd spotted her just as he decided it was safe to go in his house. *One more minute and it would've been too late.*

He missed the room. His place of security. It was almost two weeks and he hadn't cleaned up yet. He had to clean up. *Stupid bitch. Stickin' her nose where it don't belong. Ought to cut that goddam nose off and shove it down her throat.*

He knew it would never be safe to go back now. He'd have to leave it all and start over. Find another place. *What a waste. What a stupid, fuckin' waste. All because of her.*

He wasn't aware that he'd spoken aloud until a sultry voice responded. "You talkin' to me Mister?"

The voice belonged to a young, chocolate-colored girl with dreadlocks and enticing dark eyes. He shot her a venomous look. "Fuck you."

She emitted a throaty laugh, her voice now husky with disdain. "Don't you wish, white prick."

Two more hours passed without anyone showing an interest in the house. The night people slowly disappeared from the streets, pulling into their respective holes. The emptiness was eerie.

Barbara wondered how long it would take Harmon to give up. Simms was already dozing, slumped uncomfortably in a chair across the room, and she was having a hard time staying alert. There'd been no business at the station for over an hour. She didn't want to be the first to quit, but damn, this was getting ridiculous.

Just as she was about to push the button on the walkie-talkie, a car pulled into the station, stopping outside the door. The flash of lights through the large window startled Simms into instant alertness. "What?"

"I think it's Harmon." Barbara stood and stretched her aching back and shoulders. "Maybe he's ready to wind this up."

Harmon walked in and wiped a large hand across his haggard face. "Well, we tried."

"Don't give up yet," Barbara said. "We can always do it again."

"Shit. If that was him, he'll never come back." Harmon dropped coins in a pop machine and pushed a button for Mountain Dew.

"Maybe we can go to him."

Harmon turned quickly. "What do you mean?"

"I'm not sure," Barbara said. "But my gut tells me your killer is happily living and working in Twin Lakes."

"That guy you told me about?"

She nodded. "When I saw the target tonight, I thought there was something familiar about him, but I can't swear to anything."

"That does us a fat lot of good."

"Unless I put a little pressure on him, see what I can force out."

Harmon regarded her eager expression and sighed. "Do it by the book Hobkins. Don't give a defense attorney room to scream coercion."

Dawn was just beginning to cast gray-pink shadows across the landscape when he pulled into the driveway. He turned off the engine, doused the lights, and sat there. She'd come to the door if she heard the truck. That is, if she was sober enough.

Slobbering old cunt. Always whining because she didn't have enough money for booze. But drunk all the time anyway. Ought'a take it all away from her. Serve her right.

Why was stuck with her all these years anyway? He'd always thought his father was stupid but discovered later he was wrong. The old guy was pretty smart. Smart enough to walk out one day and never come back.

Years later, his sister had proved she was no dummy either. Shacked up with some rodeo cowboy and took off to parts unknown. *I should'a split, too. Left the old bitch to rot by herself. No more ridin' my ass for something I didn't do.*

It was funny. He'd never questioned his staying before. It certainly wasn't love, more like guilt that held him rooted like some old tree. Maybe her constant bitching had finally opened the door to his doubt. Maybe he *had* wanted Frank to die.

He hadn't thought of his twin brother in a long time, and this new thought frightened him. *Frank. Why'd ya hafta go and die like that? Everything would'a been okay if you hadn'ta died.*

Frank had died just one month shy of their eleventh birthday. It was the first week of summer vacation and the boys had gone to the nearby creek to play.

They made a raft out of scraps of lumber and pretended they were sailing the ocean on a pirate ship. They were so engrossed in the adventure that they didn't pay attention to the darkening sky or the rising wind. Suddenly, a loud clap of thunder exploded, releasing a waterfall of rain.

"Frank, let's get out'a here." He watched the creek swell, and his fear mounted as the swirling water tossed the raft like a piece of driftwood.

"Don't be a sissy." Frank had to shout to be heard over the howling wind and pounding rain. "We're sailors. We can ride out any storm."

"I don't wanna. I'm scared Frank. Let's go home."

Frank grinned and plunked down in the middle of the lurching raft. "Go on sissypants. I'm the captain. The captain always stays with his ship."

Then a swell of water lifted the raft and hurled it at an overhanging tree. Frank rolled across the slippery planks of wood, and his grinning face disappeared. Just like that. Gone. Swallowed by the froth of rushing water.

Staring at the spot where his brother went under, he almost missed his opportunity for survival. But some instinct made him grab a branch and cling to it as the brown water surged and tugged around him. He waited for his brother's head to bob up beside him. It seemed like he waited forever.

"Frank! Frank! You quit playin' games with me."

The only response was the scream of wind and the roar of angry water.

"Goddam you, Frank. You better come up or I'm gonna kill you."

When the realization hit, it almost cost his tenuous hold on the tree. He felt a stab of something horrible deep in his gut. Frank was gone. He was never coming back.

A part of his mind told him to let go, to join his brother in the murky depths of the water. But his arms clung madly to the slippery bark, refusing to obey.

Just as quickly as the storm had come up, it abated. The rain slowed to a steady drizzle and the creek settled into a quiet, laughing rush. He spent his last reserves of strength to pull his weak body up on the bank and lay gasping into the dank earth. He felt like a part of his very being had disappeared along with the smiling face of his brother. His final threat to Frank rang loudly in his ears.

"Oh, God!" he cried. "I never would'a hurt ya, Frank. Never!"

Hours later, when they finally found the body tangled in a mire of debris that had been collected by the raging water, he was numb with grief and fear. He kept thinking it would've been better if he was the one, not Frank.

His mother came to his room just once. She didn't touch him or offer any part of herself in shared grief. She simply stood in the doorway, coldly staring at him.

She doesn't care, he thought. *All she cares about is her booze and those pricks she sleeps with.* Once again the file began it's relentless hacking across his skull.

He was relieved when she turned and slammed the door. Later, even his sister's gesture of kindness failed to really touch him. "It wasn't your fault," she said. "I know you loved him."

Despite his sister's words and awkward embrace, all he could see was the picture of his mother's hate-filled face. She thought he killed Frank, and it would do no good to try and convince her it wasn't true.

For months, the only solace he found was in the fantasy of her body held captive by the tentacles of debris, her head smashed against the fallen trees, her worthless brains leaking out like sap, her swollen tongue protruding like a rancid balloon.

That's when he understood why his father had walked out. He could remember the screaming demands and threats she hurled like so many pieces of junk from her own sorry life. She was an ever-present, all-consuming parasite, dedicated to their misery. Frank was the lucky one, his father and Lisa the smart ones.

Well, maybe he just got his own flash of brilliance. He reached under the seat and grabbed a can of beer. His head throbbed, and that awful hacking sound filled it. In the ensuing confusion, the thoughts of his mother tangled with his thoughts of the cop.

Taking another deep swallow of the warm beer, he tried to drive the anger away, ease the pain in his head. But it wouldn't stop. It fought for supremacy as if it were a force outside him. He could see the anger as a separate entity, gaining momentum with every passing second. Like a car going off a cliff, it careened wildly off himself, his mother, and that cop.

She was getting too close. Sometimes he could swear he felt her breath warm against his neck. Knowing that, he still acted stupid. Couldn't leave it alone. No. He had to go into her apartment. Had to send those things. But she deserved it. Treated him just like his mother did. Like he wasn't worth shit. A nothing. A slithering thing under her feet.

He was smarter than she. He'd prove it.

You stupid asshole. Keep thinking like that and you've had it for sure. That kind of thinking's what got you where you are now.

His anger drained away with the last dregs of his beer and was replaced by a calm certainty. He was okay until that cop showed up. And she was harder to get rid of than a bum rap. But even her luck had to run out sometime.

He squeezed the aluminum can in a powerful grip and looked down when he felt a slight stab. A ragged piece of the metal had pricked his finger, and blood slowly rolled down the appendage into his palm. He stuck his finger in his mouth to stem the flow.

The taste was familiar and pleasant.

Chapter Twenty-Four

Saturday, November 13—Twin Lakes

Barbara couldn't remember the last time she'd been so tired. The way she felt right now, she might not make it through one more day before collapsing in total exhaustion. It was only expectancy that drove her numb body from bed into the shower. She was close. She knew it. Just this once, luck had to be with her.

But the prospect of going to the Avery house again created a mix of excitement and dread.

Slipping her Walther P-38 into its shoulder holster, Barbara felt like Wyatt Earp heading for the OK Corral. She'd only fired once in the line of duty and, luckily, the shoulder shot took the man down. Not so lucky for him as he pulled a ten-to-twenty for armed robbery, but lucky for her. She wasn't sure she could live with being responsible for cutting a life short, any life.

She hoped today wouldn't present the opportunity to find out.

Oblivious to the unusually heavy Saturday traffic, Barbara drove with automated determination toward her destination. Because Royce Wertco's life could depend on her bluff, she carefully rehearsed what she was going to say to Earl Avery.

Parking behind the familiar pickup, Barbara got out of her car and took a deep breath. Her lungs felt like jellied tissue paper, and the cold morning air drew her breath in gray shreds as she made her way onto the sagging porch. The cheap, hollow-core front door shook under her knuckles, then it was yanked open.

"What do you want?" Earl's mother asked, her face contorted with open hostility.

"I need to talk to your son."

"About what?" The woman drew her thin, food-spattered robe around her bulky body.

"Some business in Dallas."

Barbara caught the brief flicker of alarm that crossed the woman's face before she retreated to bravado again. "He don't have to talk to you about nothin'."

"He will if I get a court order. Then it gets legal. Maybe he'd like to avoid all that mess."

Barbara waited for some response from the woman, and the silence grated. She hadn't anticipated having to bluff her way in but found an ally in her mounting anger. Mrs. Avery stood rigid in the doorway while the silence stretched on.

Finally, the woman moved aside. "Get it over with."

Barbara took a quick mental inventory as she was led through the narrow entry hall. *My God, it's worse inside than out.*

To her left a doorway opened into the dining room. Barbara was amazed at how much furniture was crammed into the small space. She assumed that the other doorway at the far end of the room led to a kitchen. All along the hall, torn, stained wallpaper clung to the wall, exposing a cheesecloth-textured skeleton in spots.

She followed Mrs. Avery into the living room. One small window provided the only light. Like the other rooms, it was cluttered with massive pieces of furniture and junk. The old woman pulled a dingy string suspended from the tall ceiling, giving life to a single naked bulb that was crusted with dust and grease. The yellowish light barely penetrated the deep corners of gloom.

Mrs. Avery crossed the room and stood at the bottom of the stairs. "Earl," she called. "Get down here."

A distant door slammed and loud footsteps descended the staircase. When he neared the bottom, Barbara could feel Earl's gaze boring into her.

"Whatta ya want?" His bravado matched his mother's.

"Earl." His mother put a restraining hand on his arm. "Why don't you..." She jerked her hand away as if shocked and looked quickly at Barbara.

For a moment, Barbara was puzzled by the old lady's sudden reversal. *Damn. They're both crazy as hell.*

Earl took the last two steps slowly, keeping his eyes on Barbara. He'd seen her gaze linger on the quilt tossed over the back of the sofa. He'd also seen the flicker of interest in her eyes. Now she turned those eyes to his.

"Mr. Avery, where were you last night between the hours of ten and three this morning?"

Before he had a chance to answer, Mrs. Avery offered his alibi. "He was home all night."

Barbara glanced from one to the other, not missing the look of surprise that crossed his face. Or the smug satisfaction in the old woman's eyes that met hers without flinching. *That lying bitch.*

"That's right," Earl said. "I was here."

"How do you know he didn't leave after you went to bed?" Barbara asked.

"I don't sleep so good." The woman's rheumy eyes held Barbara's. "When I get up at night, I look in on Earl." She smiled sweetly. "No matter how old your children are, a mother is always a mother."

Barbara wanted to throw up. That woman probably never experienced a maternal feeling in her entire life. Her kind ate their young.

But Barbara also knew the woman wouldn't waver from her statement. There would be no benefit to pushing any more right now. She could only hope that this little nudge put him off balance enough to make a mistake.

"That certainly answers my question." Barbara glanced toward Earl. He remained at the foot of the stairs while Mrs. Avery stood and looked anxiously at him. The silence was deafening.

"Thank you," Barbara said, turning to leave. Then she stopped in a perfect Colombo move. "By the way, I couldn't help noticing that lovely quilt. Did you make it?" She looked directly at the woman.

"No, my mother did. We have lots..."

"Stop." Earl stepped forward and waved an arm at her. Then he turned to Barbara. "You get outta my house."

Barbara was only too happy to leave. She'd gotten the reaction she wanted.

The old woman watched until the detective's car was out of sight then marched back into the living room. *No way was he going to get away with talking to her like that.*

"I don't know what you've been up to," she said to a startled Earl. "But I'm done. This is the last time I'm gonna cover for you. You've been nothing but a whimpering slob all your life, and I'm tired of cleaning..."

A whirling confusion in Earl's head hurled her words into some soundless void. He was only aware of the twisted, ugly mouth. He moved toward her in slow-motion steps. A caldron of hate bubbled deep inside. He realized with a cold detachment that he hated her, had always hated her. Now, he knew what to do. It was so simple, why hadn't he seen it before? Take care of the old bitch then just sit back and wait. The other one would be back. All he had to do was wait.

Alarms rang through the old woman's body with each step he took toward her, but fear held her rigid. Frozen, she watched his predatory approach in fascinated horror. He seemed suspended in time, a jagged fragment of film played in an endless loop.

Then her fear erupted, and she did what any terrified animal would do. She ran.

Crowder was bent over a huge microscope when Barbara entered the lab. She'd convinced her conscience to bypass Broyles one more time. If she walked into his office with nothing but Earl Avery's frantic reaction to her visit, she'd never hear the end of it. "Chief Broyles says we need more tests on those quilts," she said to the hunched man.

Crowder didn't reply. He dialed a large black knob on the microscope, then jotted a note on a pad of paper next to it.

"This is important."

"Everything's important Detective." He finally looked at her. "What I'm doing now is important."

"I need those tests."

He wiped a bony hand across his face then sighed. "If I do them, will you get off my ass?"

Barbara nodded.

"Okay." He pointed across the room. "Stand over there. Get some coffee. Read a medical text. Whatever. Just stay out of my way."

Like a good little student, Barbara moved where he indicated. But, instead of reading, she watched him slip one slide after another under the microscope's eye. After studying each one, he stopped and made long scrawling notations on the pad. It was filling up fast.

Come on, she silently urged. She had no idea how long it would take to complete the tests she needed, but she resented every second he was using for these.

A half hour later, he motioned her over. "Okay, Hobkins. Think I've got it."

"You mean...? You've been working on my stuff all along?" A surge of adrenaline raised her heartbeat.

A look of smug satisfaction crossed his wrinkled face. "Figured I'd eliminate the hassle. I knew you'd be back." He coughed and turned back to the pile of notes. "I already started this when Broyles put the lid on. Don't like unfinished business."

Barbara was stunned. She hadn't thought Crowder possessed a shred of human kindness. She felt like hugging him. She held her breath instead, expecting the worst. "What did you find?"

"There are at least three pieces of material that match between quilt B and C. But A is still a stand-alone. I'll get this typed and..."

Barbara didn't wait to hear the rest. She whirled and headed for the door. "I love you Crowder," she called back over her shoulder.

"Don't love me," he shot back. "Just leave me the hell alone."

What is it now?" Broyles asked, irritated by Barbara's interruption.

"I got it Chief. I finally got the connection." She started to sit down but realized she was too excited. "I just came from the lab. Crowder finished the-"

"What the fuck are you doing?" Broyles came up out of his chair. "You want to get us all fired?"

"He did it on his own time." Barbara raised a hand as if she could hold back his anger. "The important thing is that two of the quilts match. The one from the Nelson murder and the one from Dallas. And, just a few hours ago, I saw another quilt. In the Avery house."

"What the hell were you doing there?" Broyles slowly lowered his bulk to the chair.

Barbara kept a close watch on his face, ready for another eruption, while she told him about the stakeout and the subsequent visit to the Avery's.

He scratched his chin while he listened, and she was relieved when he continued to sit there after she finished. Maybe he was finally starting to believe her.

"What about the Delgrave quilt?"

"It didn't match."

"Then who killed her?"

"One thing at a time Chief. Right now we're looking hard at Earl for the Nelson homicide and the one in Dallas. Once I get some of those quilts from his house, we can see what connects to Delgrave."

"Can you swear this Avery guy's the one you saw last night?"

"No. But I know it was him Chief. And the alibi his mother gave is a crock if I ever heard one." She gained confidence with the telling. "And, I bet he's the one who broke into my apartment. His little present may have been a message." She paused to give him time to digest the information, then leaned forward. "Get me a search warrant, Chief. The quilt may not be the only evidence I find."

Broyles swiveled his chair away from the intensity on her face. Watching the rise and fall of his large chest, Barbara held her impatience in check and waited for his answer.

The chair groaned under his weight as he turned back. "Okay, I'll get it."

"You won't regret it. I promise."

"Let's hope neither of us does," he said then added. "Take Reeves with you."

Barbara nodded and walked out.

Keith wasn't in their office. *Damn. He's never around when I need him.* A little checking revealed that he was signed out on a burglary case with Vaughn. "Great. That's just fuckin' great."

She was so close. If Keith came back in time, fine. If not, she'd go alone.

While she waited for the warrant, Barbara thought about calling Gene. She'd tried not to think about him in the past two days, but odd, spare moments had found her replaying that final scene. Had it just been his pain that had closed a door between them? Did they have enough of a relationship to open it again? *Maybe just one quick call.*

The school secretary answered on the third ring. "No. Mr. Wilkins isn't avail-able. He's taken a personal day."

Damn. Barbara cradled the receiver. Should she call him at home? *No.* Maybe this was a sign that it was too soon. They could talk later when she had more time. As soon as she was out from under the pressure of the job, everything would be okay. It had to be.

Chapter Twenty-Five

Saturday, November 13—Twin Lakes

Late afternoon, and already the gray limbo before dusk prevailed, giving the sky a surrealistic look. Barbara was still trying to adjust to the time change that abruptly robbed daylight and brought the darkness of night an hour earlier.

A shudder shook her when she realized she was alone and very vulnerable. The weight of her gun against her side gave small comfort. *Don't be ridiculous. You're the one always professing the ability to do anything. Handle any situation. And you could've waited for Keith.*

Properly chastised, she continued driving until she reached the house. The truck still occupied the same spot as that morning. Barbara looked at the house, rendered even creepier in the gathering shadows, and a momentary urge to turn around seized her.

What kinds of monsters are spawned in a place like this?

Shaking off the thoughts threatening to freeze her courage, Barbara turned off the engine. Then she slid out of the car, the warrant clutched in one moist hand. She strode resolutely to the door, choosing her footing carefully in the fading light. *Maybe he won't be here. It'd be easier to deal with the old woman alone*

The door's hollow groan seemed like an obscene intrusion into the silence surrounding the house. Barbara hesitated before knocking again. There was no movement. No sound from beyond the door. Now she could leave. No one was here to receive the warrant.

While her mind wrestled with her fear, Barbara's hand grasped the cold metal doorknob. It turned, and the door swung open. She couldn't see anything in the dim interior, but a cold draft blew across her face. Then another. She tried to force her eyes to adjust. A silly memory of a dark theater and the movie SCREAM crossed her mind.

Suction slammed the door shut, the sound shattering the silent house. Automatic instincts conquered her fear. *Find some cover.* Slipping into the darker shadow of a grandfather clock, Barbara eased her revolver out of the holster. She mentally counted each loud heartbeat and waited, cursing the darkness at the end of the hall. Breathing became easier when a full minute passed, and the house held its silence. Her eyes had adjusted slightly, and the blackness ahead was kaleidoscopically breaking into lighter slivers. Pieces of furniture slowly took shape in the gloom of the living room. The eerie half-light from the small window cast a puzzle of shadows, and Barbara realized there was precious little daylight left. When full darkness came, it would be sudden and complete.

Why hadn't she brought her flashlight? *Silly question now.* The silver-ribbed issue was tucked away in the glove compartment of the Datsun.

Barbara eased forward, away from the security of the clock, and made a careful circuit through the dining room. The unused area was on the north side of the house and felt ten degrees colder than the hall. She pulled her jacket tighter and made a conscious effort to draw a deep breath. The air was heavy with a dead smell. No, maybe not dead, just rotting fibers from stained carpeting and decades of dust.

The kitchen was adjacent to the dining room, just as she expected. An ancient stove, minus one leg and the oven door, stared at her: its black mouth open in a silent scream. *Shit, Hobkins. Things are spooky enough around here. You don't have to paint any more pictures.*

Unlike the dining room, the kitchen held a faint pleasant odor of pastry. The tightness in the back of Barbara's neck eased a notch. She walked to the back door and peered through grimy glass into the back yard. She never could look at a dirty window without thinking of her mother's fetish for cleanliness.

She could make a career out of this place.

The dimness of the yard and the appearance of a mottled moon lifting off the horizon, brought back an urgency. *Get what you need then get the hell out of here.*

The kitchen leaned crazily westward, following the direction of a sagging foundation. Barbara felt like she was in a fun house, the kitchen trying to spill her into another room. Her Walther felt comfortable and familiar in her hand. She'd always preferred the strength and power of a Magnum, but had grown accustomed to a little less weight in her hand.

Coming into the living room from the new direction, Barbara thought it was slightly darker than before. A chill hand of unease crept up her spine again. Then she heard a faint sound from the stairs. Or was it behind her? She stood perfectly still, straining to hear the noise again, but the house was silent.

A clock on the mantle made a soft tick, then struggled for another. Again, Barbara thought of her mother. *She would've kept the clock wound and running perfectly.*

Chasing that distraction away, Barbara swept the room with a careful eye. Like the stove, the quilt seemed to stare at her from its resting place. She removed a large black bag from her jacket pocket and dropped it on the sofa. *No sense in lugging the quilt around.* She could pick it up when she left.

Only the upstairs remained. She stood with one foot on the bottom step and hesitated. *You don't have to go up there. You can go back. Get Keith. Do it by the book.*

Not heeding her own good advice, Barbara climbed the stairs, one slow, agonizing step at a time. A door at the top beckoned with some unknown force, and she ignored the other two openings in the short hallway. Taking a deep, steadying breath, she reached for the doorknob. Hinges, thick with layers of paint, emitted a faint grating squeak. Her fingers tightened their grip on the gun as she stepped into the room.

Barbara didn't know what she expected to find, but not this... this horror spotlighted in a fading shaft of sun from a west window. A scene grotesquely stage-managed by nature herself.

Through a whirling storm of revulsion and terror, Barbara's mind took note of the things out of place in the bedroom. Dark maroon splatters running in jagged patterns down the dingy paisley wallpaper. Twisted, tattered clothing flung carelessly on the floor, soaking in dark pools the color of dying roses. Scarlet stains shockingly wiped across an aging Provincial vanity. A pitiful figure propped against the edge of the bed, clutching the end of a faded quilt in one hand.

The figure was barely recognizable as a person. Most of the face was gone, exposing the starkness of bone framed by clotted blood and pieces of crusted tissue. Where a mouth should have been was a ragged, gaping hole.

A picture of the downstairs stove flashed before Barbara's eyes. It *had* been screaming.

A whisper of sound drew her attention and, swallowing her own scream, Barbara whirled to see a hulking figure step from the closet.

"I've been waiting for you." The voice was soft, yet abrasive, paralyzing Barbara so she could only stand and watch the dark form advance.

Then she remembered the gun and raised the barrel. "Stop."

A harsh, grating chuckle met her challenge. She leveled the barrel and held steady on what she hoped was the second shirt button above the belt. The kill zone. *No shoulder shot for this guy.*

Barbara didn't see the shadow move, only a blur before she heard the sound of swiftly moving air a millisecond before the roar of her shot. Then she felt an electrifying stab of pain, followed by the crack of her wrist as it broke. Abandoning the gun, now lost somewhere on the floor, she seized a moment of confusion and ran. White-hot pain ripped through her arm. Raucous laughter followed her stumbling plunge down the stairs.

Got to get out of here. Barbara made a frantic dash toward the front door and fumbled with the latch. It wouldn't open. *Must've locked when it blew closed.*

Struggling against the rusty lock and the throbbing pain, she could hear his progress as he banged through the crowded living room. He was getting closer. She heard his heavy footsteps enter the hall.

The door refused to open.

Once again, Barbara sought refuge beside the clock, wedging her slim frame between it and the wall. She heard his rattled breathing as he drew near. *Come on, you bastard.* She counted his footsteps to keep herself from acting too soon. One more second, then she gave a mighty heave against the clock. A groan escaped her lips as a piercing pain shook her body. The clock teetered for a moment, then gave way and toppled forward, striking him across the back.

Her reactions were agonizingly slow as she skirted the downed figures of man and clock and ran toward the kitchen. *Oh, God. Let me get out.*

The back door didn't yield, and Barbara fought the impulse to give up, to give way to the horrible pain and inevitability. Resistance seemed futile. She could hear him again, smashing his way through the dining room. *It can't end like this. I won't let it.*

She ran blindly toward the living room. The fireplace was there. And a poker. With it, she wouldn't be completely defenseless.

Suddenly, she bumped into something huge and dark. A whoosh of air startled her. It was him. He reached for her with rough hands raking across her body, tearing her blouse in an attempt to hang on. Barbara lashed out with a strength born of desperation and pushed. When he stumbled back, she ran again. Her only hope was in distance. But how much distance could she gain trapped inside?

She heard him gasping for breath over soft whispers of sound as he regained his footing. Then stronger sounds as he started his pursuit again. Heavy, hollow echoes of footsteps on the wood floor came at her from the left. Faster and faster the staccato beat grew.

A cold, rational part of her mind told her it was almost over. She had nowhere to run and could count the remainder of her life in a few short sweeps of a minute hand. She thought of Susan Delgrave and the others. Their horrible last moments of life would soon be hers. *Oh, please, God. Let it be quick. And not in vain.*

Barbara turned to face her attacker. If it was the end, she wanted to see him.

A sudden white beam of light stabbed the darkness and caught the hideous face of her assailant in a sharp profile. Avery turned toward the source of the light, eyes glaring. He never knew what hit him.

Barbara didn't know either.

The light source suddenly shone against the filthy rug. There was a faint foot shuffle then a soft expulsion of air, followed by a thunderous shattering. Earl

Avery's skull exploded under the blow, shooting splintered bone fragments and torn brain tissue in a bloody froth across the room.

Barbara's knees hit the floor before Avery did. Then she recognized the other person.

"Gene. Oh, Gene. How did you know I..." The weakness of total relief took control, and she sagged forward. It didn't matter how he knew she was there. All that mattered was that he came to help.

"Gene, I'm so glad." She tried to rise. She had to take control. He was just standing there, maybe waiting for her. "It's over now. It's okay."

Still, he stood in silence.

Barbara blinked hard against the blinding pain in her arm. The flashlight lay only a few feet away, its beam shining upward, capturing Gene like a bizarre black and white photograph. He stood looking at her, holding the bloody poker in his right hand. Stroking it with his left.

"Gene. Please help me." She swallowed hard and tried to raise her knees from the floor.

"I didn't want it to be this way." His words brushed across her like a cold draft.

"I know. You had to. You had no choice."

"It was up to you. Don't you see now?" The voice cut through what was left of her nerves. The words came from Gene's lips but belonged to a stranger.

"Gene. What is it? You're scaring me." Barbara pushed unsteadily to her feet. "I've got to call the Chief. Help me."

"No."

The force of that single word stunned her.

"You should have left it alone. Let the kid take the fall for all of them."

"I don't understand." She took a step back, unconsciously reaching for the security of the wall.

"I had to do it. Don't you see?" He followed her retreat. "She was a slut. Giving that silent invitation. I had to take care of her. For Tom's sake. Before she became just like Nancy."

He killed Susan? This was insane. Barbara's fingers brushed against the wall, and she pressed herself against it.

Cold, empty eyes regarded her, and her mind reeled crazily. *This can't be happening.* She fought the confusion and looked for something, anything to protect herself with. But there was nothing. The only hope she had was to talk him out of the madness.

"Gene, let me help you. It doesn't have to end like this."

"There's no choice." He took another step forward. "You should have left it alone."

Barbara sidled away from him until she reached the corner. Part of her was detached, and she watched his face, mesmerized by the stranger she saw. His eyes were focused on the wall above her head. It was as if she wasn't there, and for one crazy instant she wondered if her presence was necessary. He was arguing with himself: distinctly different voices engrossed in a private debate.

"I thought you were the one. The only one who wouldn't fail me." He looked at the poker then at Barbara. "But you did. Don't you see?"

Suddenly, she did see. How could she have been so blind? So stupid? Had he asked for her help? Yes. Little things. Subtle mood changes and fragments of discrepancies she overlooked, all in the name of love. *Oh, God. Love.*

And Keith. He'd tried to warn her.

Barbara forced herself to look into Gene's wild eyes and forget what they had meant to her. If she had even a prayer of besting him, it would come from his eyes. They would reflect his decision to move. She watched him take one more step and raise the poker. Timing was crucial. The moment he started the downward swing, she ducked to one side. The poker crushed the plasterboard where her head had been.

He whirled, trapping her in the corner. "Don't make it harder. Just let it all end."

Barbara knew she only had one more chance. It had to be a good one. "How can you kill someone you love?"

Her words made him hesitate, and she made her move. Bracing her feet against the wall, she lowered her head and shoved her body forward, striking him in the groin. He grunted loudly and fell back, stumbling over the prone body of Earl Avery. The poker fell with a soft thump on the carpeting.

Barbara watched Gene backpedal in an almost comic effort to regain his balance. Then his body was held momentarily suspended in air before it went over backward. Seconds before his body hit the floor, his neck and head crashed loudly against the edge of the heavy oak coffee table. The force of the blow snapped his head forward.

After giving Barbara this final nod, Gene lay still, very still, beside Earl Avery.

Her dulled brain barely heard the heavy pounding and the shattering of old wood. Only the sound of Keith's voice registered. "Barbara!"

"Keith. Oh, God. Keith."

The next minutes were a blur of activity as more people rushed into the room and more lights pierced the darkness. Barbara took another look at the crumpled forms of Earl Avery and Gene Wilkins. Keith rushed over and supported her before she sagged to the floor. "It's over," he said. "It's all over.

Grateful, she hung on to his arm as he helped her to a nearby chair. When the numbness started to recede, she became aware of the Chief's voice thundering through the room, barking orders to uniformed officers. Her pain-filled eyes sought his. He gave her a brief nod. "Good work Hobkins."

Barbara sighed, closed her eyes and rested her head against the back of the chair. How could it be good when she'd fucked up so badly?

She protested the ambulance to no avail. Broyles insisted, pushing Keith into the back with her. The only consolation was that she managed to talk them out of the sirens and lights. Somehow, she couldn't justify clearing traffic for a mere broken wrist.

Keith sat across from her, discomfort obvious in the frequent pulls on his tie and his inability to hold eye contact.

"Hey, I'm all right." Barbara reached out with her good hand and touched his knee.

"I know. But damn that was close." Keith swallowed and glanced away again. "Wilkins. Never guessed about him."

Barbara's fingers tightened on his leg, and he patted her awkwardly. "Sorry," he said. "I shouldn't have brought that up."

"No." She smiled weakly. "Can't spend the rest of my life avoiding it."

"I just keep thinking of how you must feel. I mean... I know how I feel and I wasn't..." His voice drifted into another plane, and Barbara watched his lips move, yet hearing nothing.

She didn't know how she felt. For the most part, numbness ruled. Except for the throbbing pain in her arm. But what about her heart? She didn't feel anything there, and she should. After all, the man she thought she loved had almost killed her.

Barbara wasn't aware of the tears until Keith reached out and gently wiped her cheek. "You just rest now. No more talking."

"But I've got to. Before..." Her voice broke. "I heard the Chief tell you to fill out the report. There are things you have to know."

"It'll wait."

"No." She propped herself up with her good arm. "The record has to be right. For his sake."

"What the hell?" Keith forgot where he was and tried to stand, banging his head on the roof. He slumped to his seat and rubbed the pain. "He tried to kill you."

"Yeah. But he didn't." Barbara eased back down. "If he really meant to, he wouldn't have missed."

"Bullshit! What about the Delgrave woman? And that girl?"

"I don't think he killed Aimee."

"What?"

"You weren't there. Didn't hear what he said." Barbara looked at her partner, imploring him to understand. "Gene was sick Keith. But, in that sickness, he thought he was right. He insinuated that Susan was being unfaithful to Tom. Compared her to his former wife. I think that woman did something terrible to Gene and unleashed a monster in the process. But that monster didn't have a reason to kill the girl."

"Then who did?"

"Avery, I think. We'll know when we get a report on the quilt from his house. I'm sure it'll match with the one found on the Nelson girl. And Avery's the one Harmon's been after."

"A lot of sickos in the world." Keith started to reach for a cigarette then stopped. "I'm glad we're the good guys."

"Yeah, me too." Barbara closed her eyes. "Me too."

For a moment, all Barbara heard was the sounds of traffic and the tires singing on the pavement, "It's over. It's over." But it would be a long time before it was really over. She clutched Keith's hand and he squeezed back.

Epilogue

Twin Lakes

Epilogue
Twin Lakes
A week later, the county buried Gene Wilkins. Few people came to mourn him on this gray, blustery day. With her good hand, Barbara held her coat tight against the invasion of wind and watched the casket as it slowly lowered into a gaping hole in the ground. Then she walked around the mound of fresh dirt and touched Tom on the arm. "I'm so sorry we didn't get him before..."

"He was good. He had us all fooled."

They'd torn up Wilkins' back yard and found the skeleton buried under a flowerbed filled with pansies. Since they couldn't ask what happened, details were filled with supposition. The bottom-line being that he'd found murder preferable to divorce.

Nancy's parents came to claim the remains, finding some measure of relief in the knowing, even though knowing dismissed hope.

Tom touched her shoulder in an awkward gesture. "Thanks for all your kindness."

"Sure."

She watched him walk away before looking back at the hole. *Kindness. Was that what makes me so soft inside?*

Well, she wasn't feeling very kind right now. Rage made her want to kill him all over again. For what he'd done to Nancy. And to Susan. And to her.

"God damn you to hell, Gene Wilkins."

But Barbara didn't have to damn him. He'd already done that for himself. She turned and walked slowly back to her car, fumbling the door open with one hand. She had a week of medical leave. A week to pick up the broken pieces of her emotions and be ready for the next sicko who decided to spread havoc in this corner of the world.

The slow, lazy arc of a hawk against the sky caught Barbara's attention. She paused to watch him finish the circle. His flight looked purposeless, but she knew he was alert for the slightest whisper of movement. When he spotted it, he would dive. Then a quick intense strike, and it would all be over.

Was there a lesson there for her? Would anything be different if she'd kept some distance from the victims, from Gene? Would she have spotted some telltale clue from a different vantage point?

She leaned against the door and replayed the past few weeks against the dark screen of her mind, scrutinizing each moment, each move, for a mistake.

Okay. Getting involved with Gene was probably stupid. But how was I to know? Even Tom didn't suspect, and they'd been friends for a long time.

But no way had she made a mistake with the cases. Total absorption was her strength, and Uncle Jim always told her to lead from her strength.

So get your shit together, Hobkins. You've got work to do.

About the Author

Sutton Miller

Maryann Miller has a wealth of experience as a journalist, publishing in numerous regional and national newspapers and magazines. Nine of her nonfiction books have been published by The Rosen Publishing Group in New York. COPING WITH WEAPONS AND VIOLENCE In School and On Your Streets, which is in it's third printing, was chosen by the New York Library as one of the Best Books for Teens. She has also had two novels electronically published: FRIENDS FOREVER, a young adult novel, and OPEN SEASON, the first book in a mystery series. Miller won her first writing award at age twelve with a short story in the Detroit News Scholastic Writing Awards Contest and continues to garner recognition for her short stories, books, and screenplays. She placed as a finalist at the Sundance Film Festival with her screenplay, A QUESTION OF HONOR;. The script adaptation of OPEN SEASON was selected as a semi-finalist in the 2000 Chesterfield Film Company Screenplay Fellowship. FRIENDS FOREVER is a finalist in the EPPIE contest, an award for original electronically published books. She currently lives in Nebraska with her husband, but her heart is in Texas. An adventurous entrepreneur, Margaret Sutton has headed several unique businesses in the Dallas metroplex. These included production of home decorating items and a custom-design carpet sculpting business. Her clients comprised the who's who of Dallas society, as well as mid-east royalty who brought their personal aircraft to Dallas for her unique decorating touch. As a professional writer, Ms. Sutton has placed her work in several mystery magazines such as ELLERY QUEEN MAGAZINE. Still a resident of Texas, Ms. Sutton, shares her home with a pet monkey and considers herself "Willie's Mom."

More Clocktower Books you'll enjoy

You can find more exciting Clocktower Books at clocktowerbooks.com. Most of these titles can also be ordered at Barnes & Noble (barnesandnoble.com) and Amazon (amazon.com), as well as your local bookstore. If you are a fan of Science Fiction, Fantasy, and Horror, check out our free Web-only magazine *Deep Outside SFFH* at outside.clocktowerbooks.com.

Murder Online by Beth Anderson. A widowed mother in downstate Illinois teams up with Chicago police to solve the strangulation/rape murder of her daughter, True, shortly after True moved to Chicago to begin her first job. The only clue is a chat room. Her mother goes into the chat rooms using her dead daughter's identity to try and track down the killer. When she finds him, she has no idea who he is or where he is. But he knows exactly how to find her. ISBN: 0-7433-0068-8.

Devil is in the Details, The by Ariana Overton. Holidays are supposed to be a special time of year, but the holidays in this town are turning into nightmares. What is even worse is the killer is leaving no evidence behind or clues that may help the authorities catch this person. The Devil is in the Details takes you into the mind, and activities, of a serial killer with a different twist. ISBN: 0-7433-0087-4.

Too Many Spies Spoil A Case by Miles Archer. A wild romp through San Francisco in the Swinging Seventies with irrepressible Doug McCool, as he dodges bullets, police, the FBI, and too many spies. ISBN: 0-7433-0112-9.

Night Sounds by Beth Anderson. A world-class recording contract and a beautiful, hot woman - both on the same night. What more could a young jazz pianist want? Joe Barbarello stumbles into a nightmare of murder, sexual obsession, and international crime involving seven inhabitants of Chicago's Gold Coast, all of whom could have committed the murder. ISBN: 0-7433-0097-1.

Soul of the Vampire by Minda Samiels. A reluctant vampire tries to redeem himself while a forensic pathologist works with police to uncover the vigilante who might believe he's a vampire. ISBN: 0-7433-0095-5.

Tapestry by Ariana Overton. Everyone at one time or another wishes they could go back in time and change their life. The problem is, when it actually happens, the results can be surprising, dangerous, and life altering in ways we could never imagine. ISBN: 0-7433-0079-3.

Printed in the United States
37655LVS00004B/93